S0-AYZ-214

HE'S MAVERICK, AN ACE NAVY PILOT. HE'LL BREAK EVERY RULE TO WIN.

The two F-14s closed ranks, flying like gods above the clouds. "Maverick" piloted one jet fighter, "Cougar" the other. They were the best pilots there were.

Suddenly, Cougar felt a presence—he looked straight up and behind to see an incredible sight, an amazing feat of flying: an F-14 inverted, canopy-to-canopy with the Mig. For a moment, Maverick and Goose, his RIO, were staring straight into the Mig pilot's eyes, upside down. The bogey pilot acknowledged the extraordinary moment with a weak wave of the hand; Maverick's answer was one finger straight up—the middle one.

The Mig pushed negative G, hard down and away. He headed down into the clouds.

"The thrill of victory," Maverick said. The adrenaline was pumping through his body as it never had in his life!

"We've got to get down," Goose pointed out. "Our fuel's down to four-oh."

Maverick got on the UHF. "Cougar, this is Maverick. Let's head for the barn . . . Cougar . . . ? Where are you?"

For all their training, for all their cynical jokes, Maverick and Goose felt their bones turn cold when there was no answer from the other plane.

Most Pocket Books are available at special quantity discounts for bulk purchases for sales promotions, premiums or fund raising. Special books or book excerpts can also be created to fit specific needs.

For details write the office of the Vice President of Special Markets, Pocket Books, 1230 Avenue of the Americas, New York, New York 10020.

A NOVEL BY

MIKE COGAN

Based on the screenplay written by
Jim Casn & Jack Epps, Jr.

PUBLISHED BY POCKET BOOKS NEW YORK

This novel is a work of fiction. Names, characters, places and incidents are either the product of the author's imagination or are used fictitiously. Any resemblance to actual events or locales or persons, living or dead, is entirely coincidental.

Another *Original* publication of POCKET BOOKS

POCKET BOOKS, a division of Simon & Schuster, Inc.
1230 Avenue of the Americas, New York, N.Y. 10020

Copyright © 1986 Paramount Pictures Corporation.
All Rights Reserved.

All rights reserved, including the right to reproduce
this book or portions thereof in any form whatsoever.
For information address Pocket Books, 1230 Avenue
of the Americas, New York, N.Y. 10020

This Book is Published by Pocket Books, A Division of Simon & Schuster, Inc. Under Exclusive License from Paramount Pictures Corporation, The Trademark Owner.

ISBN: 0-671-61824-5

First Pocket Books printing May, 1986

10 9 8 7 6 5 4 3 2

POCKET and colophon are registered trademarks
of Simon & Schuster, Inc.

TOP GUN and Design is a trademark of
Paramount Pictures Corporation.
Used herein under license.

Printed in the U.S.A.

This novel is dedicated to
RICHARD NUZZI
who will soon be up there flying

Chapter 1

IT WAS CALM and starry at 20,000 feet. At that height, you couldn't even see the Indian Ocean below. Trouble was, eventually you had to come down from all that beauty; this was only an exercise, after all. And, after having all the airspace in the world at your disposal, you had to narrow your sights to an optimum landing speed of 120 knots, through potential updrafts and downpulls, and find a ship the relative size of a postage stamp to set down on. That was a neat little trick— setting a forty-ton jet fighter down precisely on a landing area the size of a tennis court. Had to catch the three-wire, too, so you and the plane could be in one piece that night. Just another day at the office for the Navy.

The *Kitty Hawk*, ninety-three thousand tons of aircraft carrier, was calm for the moment, its deck perfectly organized with an expert staff to help get the fighter planes in. But soon this calm would turn to organized chaos as the jets began coming down through the blackness. Then, those jets, flying purely on instruments and guts, would swoop down, with howls and roars and shrieks, not to mention a fierce wind equal to anything Nature could dream up.

In the dark quiet of the world above the *Kitty Hawk*, Lieutenant Pete Mitchell, code-name Maverick, and his radar intercept officer, code-name Goose, heard the landing signal officer working a Tomcat that was sliding into home plate:

"Power . . . power . . . don't climb . . . okay, hold what you got." The voice was as calm as a Sunday afternoon in South Dakota, but they knew the LSO was down there, gripping the pickle that controlled the landing lights as he talked calmly, calmly, calmly into his mike with a fighter barrelling directly at him.

Below decks, in the Air Operations Room, all the scopes were turning. Radar burped in gentlemanly fashion:

"Blip . . . blip . . . here's one . . . pardon me . . . *burp . . .* here's another . . . Communications had a battery of radios and teletypes going:

Clackety . . . squawk . . . paper coming out in reams with coded data on it . . . disembodied voices giving altitudes and latitudes, speeds and ranges . . . A row of tubes connected Radio Central and Combat Information Center with the rest of the ship; lights and bells and whistles sounded an occasional lively counterpoint to the blips and burps and squawks.

The carrier control approach officer was the center of it all, right now—the direct contact between fliers still coming in and the LSO up on deck. His eyes never left the radar screens in front and on either side of him; his mouth was never more than inches from the mike, whether he had it keyed on or off. Reports both spoken and written were raining on him steadily from the radar personnel on all sides; he didn't bother to acknowledge them, but they were giving him his grounding.

The squadron commander, code-name Stinger, came in and watched and listened awhile. "Who's up there?" he asked after a moment.

One of the radio operators was ready with the answer. "Two planes, sir. Cougar and Merlin, Maverick and Goose."

"Ah, yes. Maverick," Stinger said wryly. His eyes stayed on the two blips moving in closer on the screen before him.

"Unidentified plane inbound," one of the radar men said suddenly, a touch of urgency in his voice. An edge of tension, invisible but almost palpable, instantly keyed up everyone in the Air Ops room.

"Confirmed," said another voice. Stinger nodded, seeing it on the screen for himself. Immediately, the CCA opened his mike key; control had already tuned him to the F-14 Tomcat closest to the unknown blip.

"Ghost Rider, this is Strike," he said tersely. "We have unknown contact inbound, your vector zero-nine-zero for bogey."

"Got it," a new voice responded—Merlin, RIO riding with Cougar. In the other plane, Maverick and Goose listened intently and studied their instrument readouts. They were flying wing to Merlin and Cougar. "Contact twenty left at one-fifty, nine-hundred knots closure," Merlin confirmed.

The two F-14s closed ranks, flying like gods above the clouds. First the probe, then the nose of the second

Tomcat eased past its twin, and the pilots in their cockpits could see each other, illuminated by the orange glow of their instrument panels and screens. The planes were graceful. Slim fuselages swelled into huge air intakes. Twin tailbooms canted outward from each plane; horizontal stabilizers were making constant adjustments; enormous twin jet exhaust ports glowed red in the serene moonlight. They were floating in tandem, body-to-body now, with their wings swept back elegantly in high-speed flight position.

"I'll ID him, you hook 'em," Maverick told Cougar on the UHF frequency, plane-to-plane. He peeled off sharply to the right: five o'clock, high cover position.

Cougar kept his eyes focused straight ahead. On his windshield the dim glow of his heads-up display reflected the readouts of key instruments; directly in front of the stick, two CRT screens displayed data; the bottom screen was a radar sweep. Wedged between the instruments was a snapshot of a very pretty young woman holding a two-month-old baby.

"Closing fast," Maverick announced tensely. Then he reported to carrier command, "Mustang, this is Ghost Rider one-one-seven. Contact one bogey, oh-nine-hundred at fifteen miles, nine hundred knots of closure."

Cougar switched over to talk to his RIO. "Look for the trailer," he told Merlin. The inter-cockpit device could be heard only inside the plane, between the pilot and radar intercept officer. You never knew who might be listening to UHF; the ICD was, as far as anybody knew, private.

"I don't see anything," Merlin reported from the rear cockpit. He had more instruments, more panels, and more screens than his pilot, and they all showed one unidentified blip only. "Maverick, you have a trailer?"

They were in combat spread now, with Maverick one mile abeam and higher. His RIO, code-name Goose, answered. "Negative, Cougar. Looks like he's single."

"Hang back and watch for him," Cougar replied tersely. "Here comes—"

Trained as he was, Cougar was a very human guy. There was no keeping the surprise out of his voice as he identified the bogey.

"—Mig One!"

Closing at nine hundred knots, the Mig was just a speck, then a flash and roar, a knife-edge pass at three hundred feet. It rocketed past Cougar's left wing tip and disappeared.

Kicking the rudder, whipping the stick, Cougar made his F-14 dive with a turning roll. He slammed the throttle forward to Zone 5 afterburner. The sky lit up with a streak of lightning that was one hell of an angry Tomcat going after prey.

Maverick stayed back, covering Cougar's dive. Suddenly, there it was—a second Mig, from nowhere, dropping down onto Cougar's tail.

"Bogey on your six. I'm on his," he reported tersely, as he dove after them. Four jets streaked across the heavens and punched through the cloud cover. Cougar pulled out of the power dive, in something resembling a square corner, and started to climb again. He was doing 375 knots and closing on the first Mig, when something sounding like radar blips hit the headphones.

"I've got a six o'clock strobe," Merlin reported. "I think he's locked on us." There was something like wonder in his voice.

"It's a Mig Twenty-one," Cougar pointed out. "They don't have radar missiles!"

"Let's hope you're right," was all Merlin had to say.

"What *is* he doing?" Cougar asked, as much to himself as to his RIO.

"He's pissing me off," Merlin answered caustically.

Cougar swung some truly wild gyrations, cutting back and forth across the Mig's tailpipe, trying to break the lock-on. The tone grew more insistent: *blip—blip—BLIP—BLIP.*

"Can't shake him," Cougar muttered. He was putting the F-14 through some fancy paces now, owning the sky at 375 knots, turning square corners and bucking through five and six Gs, but when he came out of a buck-and-wing and looked around, there was the bogey still blipping right at him.

Maverick had been left far behind, keeping tabs on Bogey Two, but he was still in radio contact. "What's Mig One doing?" he queried Cougar.

"Maintaining course. Straight for Mustang." Mustang was the *Kitty Hawk*, home base.

"Stay with him," Merlin advised his pilot. Cougar nodded, listening intently now to the steadying tone: *BLIPBLIPBLIPBLIPBLIPBLIP.*

"That *is* missile lock!" Merlin said in alarm.

"He better be kidding," Cougar said grimly.

Maverick and his trailer were closer now, within sight of Cougar and Mig One. They were flying fancy maneuvers at top speed, Cougar unable to shake the bogey. "Lordy, Lordy!" Goose declared from the RIO's seat behind him. "Eyeball to asshole. Hope nobody gets the hiccoughs!"

"I'll lock in on him, Cougar," Maverick said. To

himself and to Goose, who heard everything, he added, "Hands up, don't nobody move."

"I'm up here too, Maverick," Cougar reminded him. "Watch out if you're gonna fire that thing."

"Roger, Cougar." And for his own and Goose's amusement, relieving some of the high tension, he added, "Okay, boys, drop 'em real slow and nobody'll get hurt."

In the lead plane, Cougar checked his gunsight. He got I.R. lock. He waited. The blips continued smooth and steady. "We're locked on Mig One. Why doesn't he disengage?"

"These guys are getting on my nerves," Merlin said quietly.

There was more riding on this than the four men involved. Those missiles, all cranked up and zeroed in on each other, were the real things.

Silence on the radios. Cougar and his Mig eyeballed it for another moment, still streaking around the sky at well over 200 knots, taunting each other and testing, and each refusing to back down . . . until the Mig abruptly dipped his wing and peeled off in a power dive that took him into the cloud cover and away.

"Ghost Rider to Mustang," Merlin reported to the carrier. "Bandits turning away."

But Mig Two was still on his tail.

"Cougar, break left," Maverick said. "Try a high G-roll underneath. Break out the bottom."

Cougar's F-14 broke left and dived into a dense cloud. The second Mig followed right behind.

"Bogey Two is on you now, Cougar," Maverick told him.

Cougar broke out through the cloud and looked

around, but he saw nothing—not the bogey, and not Maverick, nothing but stars and moonlight, now that they were above the clouds again. He rolled the aircraft, scanning the sky with a mounting sense of frustration and rage; he was a little bit frantic, too. Suddenly, he felt a presence—he looked straight up and behind to see an incredible sight, an amazing feat of flying: an F-14 inverted, canopy-to-canopy with the Mig. For a moment, Maverick and Goose were staring straight into the Mig pilot's eyes, upside down. The bogey pilot acknowledged the extraordinary moment with a weak wave of the hand; Maverick's answer was one finger straight up—the middle one.

The Mig pushed negative G, hard down and away. He headed down into the clouds.

"He's running for it," Goose reported.

"The thrill of victory, the agony of defeat," Maverick said, faking a yawn. The adrenaline was pumping through his body as it never had in his life. This was what it was all about!

"Speaking of de-feet, we gonna get ours wet unless we find a Texaco station. Our fuel's down to four-oh," Goose pointed out.

Maverick got on the UHF. "Cougar, this is Maverick. I'm getting hungry. Let's head for the barn . . . Cougar? Where are you?"

For all their training, for all their cynical jokes, Maverick and Goose felt their bones turn cold when there was no answer from the other plane.

Chapter 2

THE DISEMBODIED VOICE of the CCA down there, somewhere on the carrier, came over with static and wind
trying to hog the mike. "Ghost Rider one-one-five, this
is Mustang. WX three hundred. Three mile visibility.
Final inbound bearing three-four-zero."

"What a way to make a living!" Suddenly, there was
Cougar, coming in loud and strong. Maverick, and
Goose in the cockpit behind him, let themselves
breathe normally again.

"Hey, if it was easy, everybody would want to come
up here and do it," Merlin pointed out laconically.

The home base coach came on again: "Mustang to
Ghost Rider one-one-five. One-ten spin, forty-two
lock. Five miles say your needles."

"Needles down and left," Maverick reported.

"Concur, fly your needles," came the order.

Maverick made the adjustment. "Needles center,"
he said after a moment.

"Roger," answered the CCA. "Three-quarter miles. Call the ball."

"Call the ball?" Maverick repeated. "Damn straight I will."

But Cougar was having a little problem. He was frozen, one of the most dangerous things that can happen to a pilot in the air. He found himself unable to touch the instrument panel. His eyes, in his otherwise immobile head, kept moving to the photo of the woman and the baby—his wife and child. It was as though, even having been through all of this countless times before, Cougar had just realized what he'd be losing if he screwed up a maneuver.

"Hey, Cougar, you with me?" his RIO asked, trying not to show the concern he was starting to feel.

Cougar was quiet.

Merlin checked his instruments. "Bring it left. Bring it left, you're high," he said.

Cougar was still silent.

Trying not to sweat it, Merlin kept his voice level. "What? What is it?"

There was a painfully long wait and finally the pilot answered. "We're upside down!"

"Negative," Merlin snapped. "We're level."

"Can't you *feel* it? I'm hanging in my straps!"

"You're not," his RIO insisted. "Look at the instruments. We're right on the money!"

"Instruments break down. They're wrong. I am hanging in my straps! We're inverted!"

"That's negative, Cougar! We are fine. Trust me! Put it down."

The other Tomcat, with Maverick at the controls, was making its final approach to the tiny specks of light that winked below. The LSO was talking him in: "A little power . . . fly the ball . . . looking good . . . hold what you got . . ."

But up there at 10,000 feet, Cougar and Merlin were in real trouble.

"We're upside down! We can't land!" Cougar insisted.

"Well, we can't stay up here, either," Merlin pointed out.

Maverick's plane settled in over the ramp, ready to grab the wire, when suddenly there was an explosive blast from its afterburners, and the Tomcat roared on over the deck without touching. The startled flight deck crew watched in disbelief as it sheared off, rocketing back into the sky.

"WHERE THE HELL YOU GOING?" shouted the landing signal officer, blowing the eardrums of everybody who was equipped with phones instead of sound protectors.

"Uh . . . I forgot something," Maverick answered, a bit sheepishly.

"What the hell're you doing?" his RIO drawled at him. Goose was a Southern boy and never seemed to be rattled, although just this minute he was at least a little surprised.

"Helping the man in," Maverick said.

"Uh, huh. And what makes you think *we* can get back in? We don't have the fuel for this."

"Just get me to him," Maverick said.

"He's nine o'clock high," Goose answered hopelessly. "We're two thousand pounds low!"

Maverick pushed the throttles forward to mil power. The Tomcat soared straight up, its wings pressed back in the max position for thrust, and in seconds they were up again in that eerie, calm moonlight, looking for

Cougar. As Maverick came up on his six, Cougar suddenly inverted.

"I'm pulling up," Cougar said.

"No!" Merlin exclaimed. "Now we *are* upside-down!"

Maverick pulled up alongside Cougar's wing. His voice was calmness itself. "Hey, any of you guys seen an aircraft carrier around here?"

Cougar looked over at him, surprised. "What are *you* doing here?" he asked.

Maverick shrugged. "Everybody's got to be somewhere. Right now, we're with you, and—uh, I hate to be the one to tell you this, but you're inverted, Cougar. Roll it."

For a long moment, nothing happened. The two planes cruised the sky at 20,000 feet, close enough for eye contact, except that one was upside down and one was right side up.

"Cougar, this is Maverick. Half roll it. Now!" No more jokes. The order was sharp and clear—and urgent.

Responding automatically, Cougar rolled over.

"We're on vapor, Cougar," Merlin pointed out. "You got to put it down."

Cougar broke into a cold sweat. "It's crazy," he protested. "The instruments are crazy. We're going to have to eject."

In the rear cockpit, Merlin was sweating, too. "Maverick, tell him, will you tell him?" he pleaded. "Our instruments are okay!"

"You're straight and level, Cougar," Maverick told him.

"I'm hanging in my straps. I turn it over and I'm still hanging in my straps. What the hell is going on here?"

The panic had turned so cold that Cougar's voice was flat and almost emotionless, as if simply describing a scientific phenomenon occurring a billion light years away somewhere.

"You're not in the straps," Maverick told him firmly. "It's vertigo, that's all it is. Stay on my wing. I'll drop you off." He moved in closer until the planes were flying only inches apart.

"Maverick . . ."

"Yeah?"

"You'd better not be ragging me . . . if you're flying upside down . . ."

He could see Maverick shaking his head, but that didn't settle anything. "No joke, Cougar," Maverick assured him. "On the level. Even I wouldn't do that to you."

The two planes began the descent into the storm. Suddenly, Cougar panicked. "I'm upside down. I *know* it! I'm gonna eject!"

"For God's sake, don't do it, Cougar!" his RIO begged. "We're near out of fuel. Put it down, Cougar!"

"Cougar, you're on the ball," Maverick told him.

Cougar stared straight ahead at the heads-up display on his windshield. The fuel tank read Empty. His straps pulled at him because the weight of his body was leaning with gravity. Everything except the instruments told him that he was flying inverted.

"If I land this thing upside down . . . and I live—I'll have your butt, Maverick!"

"Lordy, boys," Goose put in with his jocular drawl, "this is no time to talk butts!"

At the approach, Maverick dropped Cougar off at the pattern and began to circle. Cougar dropped a wing and straightened. The wing dropped again and straightened. From the carrier's flight deck, the LSO recognized the approach of a pilot who was experiencing vertigo and trying to satisfy his inner ear on balance.

"Level your wings . . . easy . . . level . . . you're settling . . . fly the ball . . . easy . . ." the landing officer cautioned him.

Just as he was about to touch the ramp, a fierce wind shear drove the plane suddenly downward. "Power! *Power!* POWER!!! Wave off, *wave off,* WAVE OFF!"

Both afterburners blasted, but the F-14 horrifyingly settled tail-low toward the deck. The deck crew watched in terror as the plane walloped in toward them—forty tons of steel skidding in, out of control, at well over a hundred knots. Frantically, the crew scattered to throw themselves off the sides of the deck, trusting their lives to the safety nets that caught them off the sides.

The plane settled, standing on its engines for an interminable moment, while Cougar tried desperately to arrest its downward momentum. Sparks lit the stormy night as the Tomcat skidded across the deck. The plane hung for a moment, still roaring like a banshee, uncertain. At the last possible millisecond, the hook caught on the final wire—plucked out of the air—and the monster slammed hard onto the deck. Its right wheel crunched out and rolled over the side. The gear screeched and collapsed. The plane came to a halt in a cloud of fuel vapor and steam.

A silver-suit ran up to the seething mass, shouting into his mike, "Cougar, Merlin . . . come in, Cougar! Shut your engines down, you've arrived!"

He sprang to the cockpit. Seconds behind him, the landing crews scrambled back up the ladders from the nets to leap into action around the wounded plane. As always, speed in clearing the landing area was all-important; there was still another Tomcat up there needing to set down as quickly as possible. The fire-fighting equipment closed in around Cougar and Merlin, while the man in the aluminized-cloth suit and heavy helmet sprang up the ladder to peer into the cockpit. No one moved inside. He hit the canopy release. The Plexiglas bubble popped open. He grabbed at the rear seat harness release.

"Merlin, can you hear me? Sir!"

Nothing for a moment. Then the RIO's helmet moved slightly. Merlin's gloved hand came up to tear away the mask from his face. He looked at the ghostly silver-covered creature hovering above him and shook his head to clear it. He nodded. "I'm okay," he said. "Let's get Cougar out of here."

Silver-suit grabbed Merlin under the armpits and dragged him out of the plane. As he struggled to stand on his own feet, Merlin caught a glimpse of Cougar being pulled from the forward cockpit. The pilot seemed stunned, passive. He was in shock. Merlin pulled away for a moment and reached into the front cockpit's instrument panel area. He grabbed the snap-shot of Cougar's wife and kid. Then he allowed himself to be led away, as the firemen blasted the aircraft's hot-spots with foam.

"Clear the flight deck," came the booming order from the air boss as Cougar and Merlin were handed over to a flight surgeon and escorted down to surgery for the once-over.

A four-wheel mobile crane slammed up to Cougar's plane and slung a lifting harness down for the crew to hook up. The damaged plane would be hosed down, its wings settled back at seventy-five degrees, then the tillie crane would haul it over to the elevator, unhook, and send it down to the hangar deck for repairs.

Maverick and Goose had monitored the landing from just up above the *Kitty Hawk,* coasting as much as possible to hang onto some gas for their own set-down. "Is the deck clear?" Goose asked the LSO now, trying not to show the urgency he felt.

The filtered voice of the landing officer came through softly, soothingly. "Roger. Business as usual. Fly the ball."

Maverick dropped right on the dime. Flying a two-degree glide slope, coming in very flat, he increased the angle of attack as Goose read him the orders.

"Bring it left . . . you're settling . . . Is the deck clear?" he asked the carrier again.

"Roger, ball, little power . . . don't climb . . . okay, hold what you got!"

Goose did a quick sign of the cross. Maverick was too busy flying the plane to pray. Approaching the runway, he increased the angle of attack until he felt the hook dragging the deck. When it caught the wire, it slammed them down, hard. Still flying, they came up short twenty feet to the left of the centerline on the short run-out arresting wire. They cleared the foam-covered wreck and the tillie crane by about an inch and a half.

"Great balls of fire!" Goose was heard to remark. It went out over the loudspeaker and all the intercoms aboard the ship.

As they flamed out—*VVOOOOMMMM!*—and rolled up, cut the engines and sat there, immobile, waiting for a tow, Goose figured he might as well add a word or two of windup to the evening's fun.

"On behalf of your captain and your crew, I want to thank you for flying VF one-fourteen. And next time your plans include the middle of the goddamn ocean in the dead of the frigging night, I hope you'll think . . . of Naval Aviation."

But if Goose thought he had the last word, he was wrong. As the crew hooked them up to the tow, an extremely authoritative voice blared over the tower radio.

"Maverick and Goose report to Squadron Commander immediately."

Maverick looked back at Goose with a crooked smile. Then he shrugged. It wasn't the first time Maverick had been in trouble; might not be the last, either.

Chapter 3

EXCEPT FOR A very brief week or two when he was five, Maverick had never wanted to be anything except a jet fighter pilot. Being naturally rebellious, he actually had considered becoming a cowboy and roping steers—but it hadn't lasted. Who'd want to stay on the ground when all the man-talk you heard was about flying— flying against the pull of gravity, higher than anyone had ever gone, faster than anyone else had ever flown!

He carried a photograph of himself and his dad everywhere he went, along with his dad's Navy Cross. He was about eight, and they were standing in front of the very first F-14 ever tested.

He remembered the day the photo was taken. He and his mother and his little brother had been waiting for hours at the field. They never knew how long it was going to take, but Maverick remembered that his mother was growing really impatient.

"Can we go over to the hangar, Mom?" he asked. It was a hot day on Long Island, and Calverton was too far from the beach to be as much fun as other Navy bases where they'd lived. It wasn't even a base; it was a factory where they built jet fighter planes and tested them. The three of them were sitting in the visitors' area—plastic chairs and magazines and not much view of the airfield.

"You know you're not allowed anywhere on the grounds unless your dad takes you," his mother reminded him. His brother Barney was making airplane noises and sitting in reasonable content on the floor with his shoebox of small metal planes.

But just then the door opened and his dad's best friend came in the room; they all shouted, happy to see him, and he took them out on the field where they could watch the planes landing and taking off.

"There he goes!" Uncle Fred pointed out as the weird-looking, twin-tailed, two-man jet streaked by, high overhead, leaving a trail of vapor, like a snowy rainbow, across the whole earth. "That's your dad, boys. He's been up there for over five hours, refueled twice in the air. No sign of wearing him down yet, and that's pretty incredible for a fighter pilot with a two-point-one tail. Incredible!"

"If I'd known it was an endurance run, I wouldn't have bothered waiting," Maverick's mother said with a sigh. "We could have waved to him just as well from the beach, and stayed a lot cooler."

"He'll be down soon," Uncle Fred assured her. "He can't stay up there much longer now." Maverick was absolutely sure he sounded jealous.

The F-14 is not beautiful on the glide slope. Watching it land on the ground can make an observer's hair stand on end—especially if someone you love is inside. But

Rick Mitchell's wife and kids were Navy Air all the way, and even Barney didn't blink an eyelash when the prototype came bouncing in at 132 knots, looking as if it was going to pile up for sure.

Maverick understood, because his dad had taken the trouble and time to explain some of the problems as the tests proceeded. His dad had been really keen on this airplane; he said it was perfectly safe and they just hadn't got some of the kinks worked out yet. It would be fine landing on a carrier someday, when they got government okay to proceed with the testing. In the meantime, Maverick knew all the characteristics of the brand-new plane that made it look unstable in a ground landing:

High-pitch inertia similar to the RA-5C; float characteristics like the A-6A; residual thrust from the fan engines to keep the throttles in the lower, less responsive zones; a gust-responsive wing; side force characteristics to decrease seat-of-the-pants sensitivity to sideslip; a lateral control system (spoilers) to stair-step it with lineup corrections and diminish precise heading control; and an auto-throttle requiring considerable anticipation.

But the incredible new plane had something that nothing else before it had—Direct Lift Control. This landing aid consisted of four individual spoilers on the top of each wing. When DLC was engaged, by pushing a button on the stick, the spoilers popped up to a neutral position. They could be commanded full-up (plus fifteen degrees) or full-down (minus four-point-five degrees) with a thumb wheel on the side of the stick. There was a stabilizer input to compensate for the change in center of pressure, which in turn changed the pitch attitude of the airplane. Using DLC in conjunction with auto-throttle, the landing was no trouble at all.

Maverick—who at eight was known as Pete—wanted to run over to his dad the minute he climbed down from the pilot's cockpit, but he knew he had to wait for the men in suits and ties and the ground crew and the other pilots to come around and congratulate his dad on being the best test pilot in the Navy. Pete didn't mind waiting for that.

Thanks to another new invention, the Automated Telemetry System, his dad didn't have to spend another few hours going over and over what had happened. The government men and the Grumman executives had been able to monitor everything while it was actually happening. That left his dad free to concentrate on whatever test he was doing on that flight, while the ATS specialist monitored operating limits. An immediate readout permitted immediate repetition of the test, if required, and validated results of a good test. So the pilot could go to the beach with his family.

His dad broke through the little gang of men around the plane and came over to his family with a big grin on his face. He picked up Barney and kissed him and then he kissed his wife and then he hugged Pete and said exactly what his son wanted to hear: "C'mon, you want to sit in the pilot's seat?"

Permission granted. The young boy, who already had memorized all the instruments and controls, checked carefully to see if they had added anything since he had been allowed up here the last time: left side console, left vertical console, left knee panel, left instrument panel, left front windshield frame, center panel, right front windshield frame, right instrument panel, right knee panel, right vertical console, right side console.

Sixty-six controls, buttons, switches, levers, indicators, handles, pumps, and screens, and he could name them all.

"Come on, son, your mother's waiting," his dad said, grinning down at him from the step outside the fuselage.

His mom and Barney had come alongside the plane, too, and his mother had her camera out. She took pictures of Barney with his arms outspread in imitation of the F-14 in flight; of Uncle Fred standing alongside the plane; one of his dad lifting Pete out of the pilot's cockpit, and one of the two of them on the ground in front of the long, smooth nose of the plane. That was the picture Maverick carried in his wallet and set up on his bedside table at night so he could see it first thing in the morning; that was the picture he stared at for long moments sometimes, wondering what really had happened to the hero that his dad had been.

When trouble broke out in Asia again, Rick Mitchell had to go. It wasn't that the Navy insisted, because only the best pilots could be test pilots, and they were critical to the overall effort, too. But he was a man who needed to be *on* the line, not behind it.

His sons were twelve and eight when he flew a mission from which he did not return. Uncle Fred and his wife, Aunt Sally, came to the house with two other officers that Pete didn't recognize, and they sent him and his brother out of the room. Barney started to cry, as if he knew. A few minutes later, their mother called them to come in and she told them their dad was dead. She said that he was a hero, that he had died bravely for his country, a Navy hero. A few weeks later, a package was delivered to the house. It held a black leather box with purple velvet inside, and a small, gold Navy Cross. Maverick's mother gave it to him.

"If you still want to be a fighter pilot, then this should remind you what you have to live up to," she told him. "Your father was the very best. You just do the best you can at everything, too. He was very, very proud of you, and you should be proud of him, too. Always."

Why did she have to say that? There was something wrong. Something about the way his dad had been killed. There was no citation with the Navy Cross, no ceremony in Washington, D.C., and no big speech about what a hero his dad had been. Other kids whose fathers had died went to Washington, sometimes even to the White House, and admirals or the President of the United States shook their hands and told them what heroes their dads had been. But Rick Mitchell's Navy Cross, no matter how often Maverick polished it, seemed tarnished, somehow.

When he was older, he tried to find out. But even after he finished Basic and OTS and PTS and was flying the perfected F-14s himself, there was no access to any information about the night his father was killed. When the Navy closed a book, it stayed closed.

All Maverick could do was try to become as good a pilot as he could. He wasn't trying to compete with his dad—that was impossible. A dead hero was unreachable, and his dad was the biggest hero in history to him, no matter what shadow had fallen on him at the end. Every once in a while, he'd meet some old salt who had flown with his dad ten years before, or more, and Maverick would ask questions, but they never could give him the answers. Couldn't—or wouldn't.

Maverick figured maybe that had something to do

with his problem of not being able to follow rules as closely as he was supposed to. He had started getting into trouble about the time his dad was killed. Something almost always got into him and said, "Regulations don't pay off, they don't know how far you can push this plane till you've done it, they won't reward you after you're dead. Push now, do it your own way, nobody but you knows how good you are. Faster, higher, farther than anybody else—push it and to hell with their ground rules. . . ."

Teachers didn't know what to do with him. He had a great time in high school, discovering girls (they liked him) and joking around, not hitting the books much unless the subject was something he cared about, skirting disaster all the time with D-minuses or As. Teacher after teacher called him incorrigible, but they had to pass him because he came up at the last minute with the test score, the term paper, the right answers crammed—with the help of a pretty girl or an all-night study binge. When he finally got into the Navy, he settled down . . . for a while, anyway. Then he took his measure and knew how good he was alongside the others, and the maverick pony started kicking up his heels again; he couldn't help it. His nickname became official. There was more than one instructor along the way who wanted to see him wash himself out. But he was good, and he knew just how good, too. If they ever gave him a medal, they were damned well going to have to deliver it with fanfare and brass bands and the President of the United States himself was going to say, "Maverick, you're the best, the whole free world is proud of you. . . ."

What crap. He didn't care about any of that—he only cared about flying.

≡≡≡≡ Chapter 4 ≡≡≡≡

COMMANDER TOM OTAWOCZEK, better known even to his wife as Stinger, was pondering over what to do with Maverick. After that hair-raising exhibition of changing his mind about landing at the last minute, jeopardizing his life and his RIO's, not to mention the entire complement of men and planes aboard the flight deck of the *Kitty Hawk,* any other pilot would be summarily dressed down and warned. Nothing the squadron commander would enjoy more than swatting that big-headed punk kid down, and what he'd just pulled was reason enough. Except for *why* he'd done it. And how it had turned out.

Maverick had saved another pilot's life, that much seemed certain. Not just another pilot, but the best in the squadron. Vertigo can hit any jet pilot at any time; its been the cause of many terrible finales. Cougar was a fine pilot and losing him would have been a great tragedy. He was lying in sick bay, right now—instead of drifting downward in the endless fathoms below them or floating out there in the sky someplace where Air

Sea Rescue might not find him—because another pilot had risked his own life to bring him in.

What in the hell could you do with a do-it-my-own-way pilot who was as good as Maverick and as dangerous?

Nothing, this time. Again. Stinger sighed and turned to happier news. When Cougar recovered from his ordeal—and that would be tomorrow morning, when the sleeping pill wore off—he was going to get the best news of his career. Their squadron had been honored—with an invitation from Top Gun School to send their best pilot and his radar intercept officer out for special training, to challenge themselves against the best from seven other Navy squadrons. Cougar was their best. Well—Maverick in fact might be the better pilot, but he was too damned independent, not someone to represent this squadron. No, it would be Cougar and Merlin, and they'd have a good chance to emerge top Top Guns, too.

Stinger put the paperwork aside, rubbed his eyes, and thought about packing it in for the night. The *Kitty Hawk* was finally quiet, and his tiny office was becoming claustrophobic. Gray walls, gray pipes, gray desk, gray chair, gray filing cabinet, and his own gray hair sometimes made Stinger weary beyond words. He hadn't started aging until he'd had to stop flying; a desk job, even on a carrier, could make you old faster than anything. He envied those kids—but what the hell, he'd been one of them, himself. He had flown four-engine bombers and switched to fighters and then to jets—he'd had the best years in the air, and no regrets. No envy, either. He wouldn't want to be going through what Cougar must be feeling right now, with a disabled plane in the hangar deck and self-doubt giving him the shakes. Oh, well, he'd feel better than right again when he got the news about going to Top Gun. . . .

His musings were interrupted by a single rap on the door.

"Come in."

It was Cougar, a bit unsteady on his feet, due to the knockout drops.

"Cougar, you should be in sick bay. What's on your mind?" Stinger spoke gruffly, a habit. That way, nobody ever knew what he was thinking.

The tall young man, blond and deeply tanned, took a deep breath and, holding himself erect with all the strength he could muster, walked over to the desk. His eyes were glazed from the medication, but his jaw was firm.

"My wife and kid," Cougar said. He opened his clenched fist and tossed a metallic object onto the skipper's desk. The lamplight caught the gleam of gold as the hard-earned wings skidded across the polished surface and clanged up against a half-filled coffee mug.

Stinger stared at it, but he said nothing. He looked up at the young pilot, who turned and left the cabin. Stinger let him go. Cougar left the door open. Out in the hall, he almost collided with two other officers in the narrow passageway.

"Cougar!" Goose called out, surprised to see him there.

Cougar stopped and turned around. "Thank you both," he said quietly, and turned away again, making his way unsteadily down the long tunnellike passage.

Puzzled, Maverick called out, "Cougar?"

From inside his office, Stinger barked out an order. "Maverick, Goose—come in here."

No time to wonder at Cougar's curious behavior.

They stepped inside the skipper's cabin and stood at attention.

"Sir?" Maverick signaled.

The skipper didn't answer. He seemed to be keenly interested in a pile of papers in a corner of his desk. The gold wings caught Maverick's eye; he glanced at Goose to direct his eyes that way. Goose stared and shrugged his shoulders in surprise.

Finally, Stinger looked up and began to address them directly. "You just did an incredibly brave thing," he said. "But what you should have done was to land your plane. You don't own that plane, the taxpayers do. Now what *I* should do is ream you both out for it. But I've done that before. It just doesn't work with you."

Maverick shifted a bit on his feet. Getting scalded was something of a habit, but not knowing what was coming made him a bit uncomfortable. The skipper was staring at Goose; then it was Maverick's turn to come under the eye.

"You're a hell of an instinctive pilot," the skipper went on. "Maybe too good. You've never really stepped in it yet." He paused. "So this is your chance. I'm gonna send you up against the best. You two are going to Top Gun training."

Maverick was practically in shock. He had expected flak, maybe even explosions, but getting sent to Top Gun was like a reward for good behavior. It was a chance to pit himself against the very best pilots in the whole damned world, a dream he'd had since he was a kid. He'd never thought he'd qualify. Oh, he was good and he knew it, but his attitude was not always what you might call strictly military, and he'd been told a dozen times that being independent wouldn't get him into Top Gun—now, suddenly, he was in! He almost missed the rest of Stinger's speech, but then he heard Cougar's name and what the skipper was saying about him. It brought him back fast.

". . . best pilots in the world are Navy pilots. For five weeks you're going to fly against the best of the best. Cougar was going, now he's not."

"It was raining snakes up there. Cougar's a good pilot," Maverick argued.

"Only if he believes it," the skipper said. "You talk a man into flying and you lose him three months later. It's his decision. Cougar's out, you're in."

Maverick bit his lip to keep from protesting. Stinger was right, of course. It was just damned crazy. And wrong, somehow, even if it was right.

"You know, Maverick," the skipper went on, "you might have been picked for Top Gun first, yourself. Except for one thing." Suddenly he was screaming at the top of his lungs: *"YOU JUST CAN'T SEEM TO FOLLOW ORDERS!"*

Maverick stood silently at attention, Goose at his side. This was more like what they were used to.

"Maybe they'll knock that shine off your eagle and you'll see, finally, where discipline and teamwork fit in." Goose and Maverick exchanged a look. Stinger pushed his chair back and stood up, moving around the desk to face Maverick from four inches away, to go on with his little talk eyeball-to-eyeball.

"Just remember—you are representing this squadron," he growled ferociously. "If you don't graduate, don't come back. That is all. Tell me about the Mig some other time."

"Yes, sir!" Maverick agreed. He snapped off a salute and did an about-face.

"Gentlemen!" Stinger barked.

"Sir?" they answered in unison.

The skipper's facade cracked a bit, although anyone would have to be really skilled and experienced to notice it. "Good luck," he said.

"Thank you, sir."

"Thank you, sir."

Outside Stinger's cabin, they barely had time to grin incredulously at each other before they were set on by a swarm of young officers firing questions and grabbing at them to shake their hands, pummel their shoulders, touch their glory in some way for themselves. They were part of a team and the team had just won the pennant because of them. On to the World Series!

"Hey, Goose, was it really a Mig?"

"What really happened up there?"

"How close did you really get to him?"

"What did he do?"

"Some flying, Maverick!"

"Did you get close enough to see the reds of his eyes?"

"What'd he look like, Goose?"

"What'd he fly like?"

"Is he as good as we are?"

"How'd you get rid of him?"

"Was he going to push the button?"

"Did he really have you zeroed in?"

"Some flying, guys!"

But even the Mig seemed minor now that there was Top Gun to look forward to. The cadre of officers pushed their way toward the mess, where, over a hearty dinner, Maverick and Goose told the big news.

In the awed silence that hit for a second or two, a lieutenant named Culver stood up to raise a toast. "To the Ghost Riders," he said. "The best damned fighter pilots in the world—and to Maverick and Goose. Oh, what the hell! Everybody deserves a chance!"

General laughter cut the tension and momentary envy and brought back the good team spirit. Every flying officer in the mess naturally wished that *he* could have been chosen. Some had to wonder at the choice. But everyone was genuinely proud and glad that Maverick and Goose were going.

"Good luck," Culver finished lamely, downing his wine to the sounds of cheers and laughter from all.

"Pinch me, Maverick," Goose muttered. "Is this possible?"

Maverick considered it solemnly, then nodded. "It is," he pronounced. Then he drained his glass of wine and attacked the last remains of his steak.

Goose shook his head. "Me? Nick Bradshaw from Buck Holler, Tennessee? I'm going to Top Gun?" He really was a country boy, but he had gotten himself to Annapolis and his "aw-shucks," down-home drawl fronted for a brilliant intelligence that made him the best radar intercept officer Maverick had ever known or heard of. Still, every now and then Goose opened his big, friendly mouth and lifted his shaggy eyebrows and scratched his every-which-way head, and there was the Buck Holler boy all bustin' with wonder at what this "danged old world" had to show.

Goose leaned over to Maverick, in the midst of the crowd, to say, "Hey, Mav? I've got to tell somebody."

Maverick nodded. They made their way out of the mess, shaking hands, laughing, accepting bad jokes and heartfelt good wishes, and working their way out of the room, down the passageway and down two decks to sick bay. Cougar was not asleep, but he was more relaxed than they had ever seen him. He said he was absolutely sure that he knew what he was doing; the decision was the right one for him. He was truly glad for them, this they understood. Maverick and Goose came out of the quiet room and grinned at each other with excitement that couldn't—wouldn't—be contained. Goose led the way with his long strides, down the passageways, up the ladders, through the hatches, straight through to the flight deck.

They pushed open the hatch and scrambled out onto the deck, gripping the safety lines, to make their way to a fragile-looking catwalk, cantilevered high over the roiling black water. Hand over hand, they struggled to the bow of the ship, to stand at the very peak.

They yelled their news, at the top of their lungs, into the night. Maverick raised his fist in an exultation of joy. Laughing, the two made their way back into the ship for a bottle of celebratory beer.

Chapter 5

THEY WERE TO report to Miramar Naval Air Station in three days' time. That gave them a day and a night in San Diego, which turned out to be quite a night and was why they were in something of a hurry on Day Three at 2:55 P.M. on a road that crossed from the beach, through a lot of desert, to the base. There was a lot of sand on the desert, one whole hell of a lot of sand, and it was getting kicked up pretty well by the turbo bike.

It was a pretty big bike, and it rocketed across the desert as if wanting to let go of gravity, altogether. Leaning low across the handlebars, his face half-hidden by aviator shades, Maverick felt the power of the thing revving up and up and up while the road turned into a jetstream behind them. Goose hung on in back, helmet and goggles not anywhere near hiding the huge, happy grin that lit up his gaunt farmer's face like a gleeful jack-o'-lantern.

The turbo cranked faster, the screaming engine

ready to explode—higher and higher, it couldn't go any higher . . . but it did and it did again, roaring by and away, leaving dust kicked up and visible for miles. Nothing could stop this kick, the feeling of speed you got on the ground was different—and the high-pitched sound of the siren trailing them was different, too. No California Highway Patrol cops up there.

It took awhile to slow down, and then they stopped, and there was total silence out there in the desert, except for the hiss and pop of hot metal cooking in the 105-degree afternoon. Maverick and Goose sat on the bike and waited. The CHP took his time about catching up with them and getting off his bike and coming over to them. Maverick threw his leg over the saddle and stood at attention. Goose hesitated for a second, then joined him.

The cop was the portly—you might even say beefy—type, red-faced from the sun and probably with a bad digestion. He had on that arrogant but super-civil look they must learn in highway patrol school. This time it was tinged with a kind of awed disbelief. He spaced his words slowly, for effect.

"Son . . . do . . . you . . . know . . . why . . . I . . . stopped . . . you?"

Maverick answered politely. "Yes, sir. I do, *sir.*"

The CHP adjusted his own aviator glasses and waited for what seemed a very long time before deciding to pursue the dialogue. "Well . . . what . . . *is* . . . it?"

"Sir. You are going to give me a warning, *sir!*" Maverick was more than sincere.

The cop quickly suppressed a smile that would have given away his disguise as a superhuman. "I trust you have a license and registration?" he asked coldly.

Maverick handed them over, along with his Navy ID.

The highway patrolman scanned them, hesitating a minute over the ID. Maverick was almost certain he looked at him with more respect after that. "Lieutenant, do you know how fast you were going?" he asked more or less politely.

"Yes, sir. I do, *sir*."

The CHP nodded. "Well?"

"Sir," Maverick responded, "I was going Mach point one-five."

The cop nodded sagely. "One-sixth the speed of sound," he pointed out.

"Yes, *sir*."

The cop looked around Goose's lanky legs to squint at the bike. Then he turned back to Maverick. "Lieutenant . . . what . . . do . . . you . . . usually . . . fly?" he asked sardonically.

"F-Fourteens, *sir*."

There was now definitely a trace of real respect in the CHP's voice. "Tomcats?"

"Yes, sir!" Maverick answered.

There was a long pause. The cop tapped Maverick's Navy ID card on the handlebars of the still-sizzling bike. He stared at the very sincere young man with the short, straight black hair, the all-American face, the honest eyes. He shook his head and sighed audibly. "Lieutenant . . . is there . . . possibly . . . a Russian attack?" he asked finally.

Maverick was quick to respond. "No, sir. But you have to be ready."

The cop honestly didn't know if his leg was being yanked or what. He kept staring at Maverick's nice, clean-cut face, and then at the ID, and a glance or two over at Goose, the silent passenger with the simple look. Then back at Maverick—earnest, sincere, reverent. After a long time, he made up his mind as to what he'd do with these young heroes who'd broken the laws of California.

About an hour and a half later, the guard at the gate to Miramar Naval Air Station was treated to the sight of a huge turbo bike with two characters on it riding about as slowly as they could go and still stay upright. It seemed to be the escort for a California Highway Patrol car cruising along behind it, all flashers go. Or maybe it was the other way around—the CHP escorting the bike—the bikers were all "duded up" with campaign hats and fancy shades, but they were driving as if it were their first time without training wheels.

They dorked past the hangar with the sign: FIGHTERTOWN, USA. Then they pulled up at the gate. Maverick and Goose saluted the guard and handed over their identification. Behind them, the patrol car turned off its flashers and the CHP stepped out. He leaned against his door.

"Lieutenant," he said, and waited.

Maverick turned to him. "Yes, Sergeant," he answered.

"Remember one thing," the CHP said.

"Yes, sir!"

"Outside . . . this . . . gate, *I* am Top Gun."

Maverick saluted. "Yessir, *sir!*"

The CHP returned a snappy salute, got back in his car, and drove off. The guard handed Maverick and Goose back their IDs and clearance, and they turned into the base. A couple of pilots in flight suits had been on their way somewhere but, attracted by the parade, had stopped to watch and listen. One was stocky, nondescript; the other towered above him—a super specimen of tall, blond muscle. Incongruous against the zipped-tight G-suit, leg restraints, and survival vest, the *Wall Street Journal* was tucked under the flier's arm. As Maverick and Goose passed by, the cool, tall drink of water spoke, meaning to be overheard. "This one must be a real killer," he scoffed. The other pilot grinned widely, right at them, sort of a greeting—or maybe not. Maverick stared over his sunglasses at them, guiding the bike on past. Genial Goose just grinned back, happily accepting the challenge, if that was what it was.

The barracks were standard, single rooms no bigger than the Navy thought you ought to get used to. Bed, desk, chair, and lamp. Closet, chest of drawers. They were at opposite ends of the long corridor. They unpacked their duffel bags and went to inspect the rest of the layout. Class schedules and flying times were posted on a bulletin board. They were glad to see plenty of flying time—including hours of combat practice every day. The next few weeks would be crowded with classes, study time, gym and track workouts, flight simulator time, technical-update lectures, new-instrument practice, more lectures, and three meals a day.

"Hey, not much time to get into trouble," Maverick commented.

"Oh, you'll find a way," Goose reassured him.

The first class was due to start in ten minutes. They found their way to the main assembly hall of the building that housed their group. Sixteen chairs had been set up to face a giant monitor. They took the last two seats just as the lights went out and the screen lit up with fighter planes from the Vietnam time—F-4s and Mig 17s. A loud soundtrack of the Doors competed with the roar of the planes and the screaming SAMs, the exploding flak and bombing runs, filmed by gun cameras, edited so that it seemed to get all points of view at once.

Over the battle sounds, rising above the music track, an authoritative baritone voice suddenly took over the room.

"During the Korean War, the Navy kill-ratio was twelve-to-one. We shot down twelve of their jets for every one of ours. In Vietnam, this ratio fell to three-to-one. Our pilots depended on missiles. Going into that action, they had lost some of their dogfighting skills."

Now the screen changed. F14s appeared, fighting with F5s. The men in the room began to grow restive in their seats; here was something with which they identified to the marrow of their bones. The music changed, too—today's top ten crashed out to pump the blood even faster.

"Top Gun was created to teach ACM," the instructor went on. "That's Air Combat Maneuvering . . . dogfighting. Let me tell you that there were some great fighters in their day who would envy us now— Richthofen, Guynemer, Rickenbacker, Galland, Rudel, Bong . . . you know those names. Well, we do just what they did, but we do it beyond the speed of sound."

He let that sink in while the film and music roared to a climax. Then he pressed his remote button and the screen went blank. "By the way," he said pointedly, "by the end of Vietnam, our kill-ration was back up to twelve-to-one."

The lights went on, and as eyes adjusted, the fliers turned in their seats to get a look at the owner of the commanding baritone. He was stocky and muscular, with reddish hair and a scowl that looked as if he meant it. He stood near the back of the room at the console that controlled the projection.

But it was the man sitting in a chair at the back of the room, quietly returning their stares without expression, who drew their attention. He had the kind of presence to whom attention is immediately drawn when he enters a room. Tough and quiet, he commanded by just being there. The temptation to keep staring was almost as strong as the absolute knowledge that you'd be way out of line if you did.

"My name is Jester. I am your squadron leader here," the instructor's deep no-nonsense voice boomed out, as if still competing with the hard rock sounds. "Now I'd like to introduce our commanding officer at Top Gun . . . Viper."

The CO walked slowly to the front of the room. Every head turned to watch him. He was a man in his late forties, once wiry, now more on the muscular side, every ounce of it working. This was a man who would never complain, compromise, or condone. No quarter asked and none given, not with this CO. A tough cookie.

He spoke carefully and quietly, the way he had moved. "You're here because you are the top one percent of all naval aviators."

The class—sixteen young men making up eight flight crews—sat at attention. They were trim, fit, and confident: high school heroes, college jocks, who had gone on to prove themselves in the toughest game of all. These were the winners, the fittest who had more than just survived. They were the best and they knew it. The smartest ones among them also knew they still had a lot to learn, that there would always be someone very like themselves coming up behind for the kill. They listened with total attention.

"You're the elite," Viper went on, "the best of the best. While you are here, either your rear end or your brain or both are going to be moving every minute. We're gonna make you better. Because your job is damned important."

He paused, looking around slowly at each of the sixteen young and earnest faces.

"With the tensions in the world today, the potential for confrontation is greater than ever, and Navy carrier pilots will be the first ones there. Anywhere. Air combat excellence is essential."

Maverick, concentrating hard on the CO's words, suddenly had the feeling that eyes were on him from offside. He glanced over. A few seats away, a too-handsome, yellow-haired smoothie was whispering to the *Wall Street Journal* dude who had greeted them on their arrival at the gate. You could get chills just looking at the ice-blue eyes of that one. Both fliers were looking over at Maverick—Ice Eyes getting the low-down on the competition, that was all. Maverick half-smiled and turned his attention back to the CO.

". . . Someone once asked me if training men for air combat made the world less safe. Flying loaded guns, an accidental confrontation. My answer is that the really dangerous thing is being unprepared. It is dangerous when you can't do what you say you can . . . or when your opponents doubt your abilities. We don't make policy. Civilians do that. We are the instrument of policy, the tip of the spear. We had best be sharp."

Maverick looked over his shoulder again, meeting the cold and hostile stare still focused right at him.

Goose nudged him sharply in the rib. "Pay attention!" he whispered.

"Look at that guy," Maverick whispered back.

"Look at the CO!" Goose hissed, eyes straight ahead.

But apparently Viper had finished his pep talk. He stood there with his hands on his hips and looked them over. The fliers rustled and started to murmur among themselves. Maverick spoke out loud, turning in his seat to face Ice Eyes straight on. "I'm just wondering," he said, ostensibly to Goose, but too loud, "just wondering who *is* the best." That said, he turned back partway, to look at Goose again.

But, abruptly, he was face-to-face with Viper. Startled, caught like a naughty schoolboy, he grinned nervously. The CO smiled back. "If you want to know who's best," he said (with every ear in the room listening again), "we've got that plaque on the wall over there, with the *top* Top Gun crew from each class. You think maybe your name's going to be on it?"

Maverick knew when he was in trouble. He could answer for the benefit of social popularity, or he could tell the truth. He might have to take on every eager pilot in the room, but he answered what he felt. "Yes, sir."

Someone let out a surprised whistle; there were a lot of *oh*s and *ah*s bouncing around the room from the fliers. The instructors standing reverently behind the CO stared at Maverick, as if they couldn't wait to put him to a test or two. It was a bit uncomfortable, to say the least. Viper's weathered, tough-but-fair face was still leaning down into his.

"That's a pretty arrogant attitude . . . considering

the company you're in," Viper said. He got a light sprinkling of laughs.

"Yes, sir," Maverick said, somewhat less arrogantly than before.

For a long minute, nothing happened at all. Then the CO nodded, as if he'd thought it over and come to a decision. "I like that in a fighter pilot," he said. Some of the other fliers in the room did laugh then, letting the tension out, maybe. "It's okay to be confident," Viper continued, stepping back now to widen his focus onto the entire class of sixteen. "You *have* to think you're King Kong to want to try to land on carriers. Just keep in mind that when the battle out there is over, we're all on the same team."

The CO walked down the middle aisle and to the back of the room. The lecture was over. The men relaxed. Then Viper turned back to make sure he hadn't dulled the fighting edge. "Gentlemen, this school is about combat. Remember, there are no points for second place. Dismissed." He walked out of the room.

Maverick was getting a quizzical look from Goose. He grinned at him. "Do I embarrass you, old buddy?" he asked.

"Hell no. Amaze might be more like it. Astound and continue to amuse. Let's go have a look at that plaque."

Most of the other fliers were milling around it, too. A big, friendly, bearish pilot spoke up with a Midwestern flat-out drawl. "A damn plaque? I got one of those for cleaning my teeth in Cub Scouts."

"It's more than just the plaque," someone pointed out. "The winner can get asked to be an instructor."

The bear smiled blissfully. "Get to fly *every day*," he said, sighing. "Now, that's worth cranking up for."

They moved in closer to study the engraved names. Talking to the future, Goose murmured, "There's two *O*s in Goose. . . ."

That seemed to rouse up the competitive juice of the teddy bear, who turned out to be named Wolfman. He stared Goose up and down as if he'd stepped in something. Making friends was not what this finishing school was going to be about.

Chapter 6

To EVERYTHING THE "best of the best" already knew, Top Gun School was adding at last a dozen more. Technical problems were thrown at them, emergency situations simulated, reviews in calculus and virtually every branch of math and engineering were assigned and tested daily, new research and development findings were analyzed and digested, every combat situation anybody had ever encountered or dreamed up was reenacted, the physical sciences, communications skills, and a couple of new theories of aerodynamics were thrown in just to keep them on their toes for the first few days. Groundwork preparation for the big payoff—time in the air. Actual flying time would increase daily, they were assured; by the end of the term they would be at it as many hours as they could physically endure.

In those first few days, they were building foundations for something else, equally a part of being a flier—teamwork. No matter how anyone felt about competing and coming out number one over everyone else, no man ever got an airplane off the ground without some help from someone. There were two Wright brothers, and two men in an F-14, and another plane flying in tandem, and men on the ground or the carrier who keep the aircraft in flying shape . . . it might not be a popularity contest, but Top Gun men had to trust each other as well as compete. So friends were made, after all.

Anyway, no one could resist Goose. Long and lanky, easygoing, always bright-eyed and smiling, the country boy picked up friends quicker than a dog gets fleas. Maverick knew his own bravado manner tended to put people off, so he had evolved a policy of letting Goose make the friends, and then he'd go along till they noticed he wasn't so bad, after all.

By the time Wednesday rolled around, Animal Night at the "O" Club, four pretty good friends hit the place together. The guy with the perfect profile, whose good looks made him the butt of a lot of kidding, was code-named Hollywood. He took the jibes with re- signed good humor, and could dish it out as well as take it. His RIO was Wolfman, the teddy bear with a bite.

There were fast cars crowding the parking lot and driveway, and loud, fast music blaring out into the night when the four of them got there. Maverick and Goose had teamed up with Hollywood and Wolfman. The club was really jumping. Before they opened the door, the ear-blasting sound enveloped them like a thunderhead cloud.

"Okay, it's my turn, right?" Goose hollered over his shoulder to Maverick as they approached the entrance.

Maverick nodded. "Okay. Your turn."

Goose pretended to be thinking, although he had figured it out right after the last time, when it had been

Maverick's turn and things had gotten almost out of hand. "Okay, let's see," he mused out loud. Hollywood and Wolfman were half-listening, more interested in two very attractive ladies who had just walked through the door.

Goose didn't miss them, either. "Okay, let's see," he said, grinning. The bet is twenty bucks, and the gag is—you gotta have a lady . . ."

Maverick shrugged.

". . . on the premises," Goose concluded loudly.

Wolfman and Hollywood turned their full attention back to Goose with sudden, keen interest. Maverick looked dismayed.

"In the *bar?* C'mon, Goose!" he protested.

Goose shook his head emphatically. He turned to go inside. "Deal's a deal," he called back over his shoulder. "It's my turn to call it." They followed him inside, further conversation impossible against the pulsing of the hard rock beat that engulfed the bar. Under the speakers that lined the walls, plaques of the various flying squadrons hung everywhere. An old-fashioned juke box was pushed against one wall. And the place was packed.

The WOXOF bar was, of course, a steam release for people under pressure. The people in this bar were pilots and Naval officers—a careful observer would note the absence of the usual bar types. The few women present were attached, one way or another, to the Navy as well as to the men. Under the blare of the music, the talk was all about flying or hustling girls.

Goose was greeted warmly here and there around the room. He exchanged friendly insults with one officer after another as he and Maverick worked their way around the bar. They found a landing place and ordered a couple of beers. "Hey, there's Keller, Black Lion Squadron," Goose said. "He's damned good."

"Is there anybody in the Navy you don't know?" Maverick asked.

"You forget I am a bona fide *ring-knocker*," Goose said proudly. He knocked his Annapolis ring on the bar. "I knew a lot of these geniuses at the academy. Besides, I'm the RIO—I gotta keep track of the competition, don't I? Part of my job." Suddenly, he turned and stuck out his hand to grab someone passing by. "Slider!" he exclaimed. "They let you into Top Gun? If you're the best in the Navy, I tremble for the security of this country."

The shaggy-headed young officer stopped, peered at Goose, and shook his head woefully. "Goose! Whose butt did *you* kiss to get here?" he asked.

Goose grinned his easy, "aw-shucks" country-boy smile. "The list is long," he acknowledged, "but distinguished."

"So's my Johnson," Slider said.

"Who's your pilot?" Goose asked him.

Slider stood an inch straighter. "The Iceman," he said proudly.

"Iceman, who's that?"

Slider nodded his head toward the starboard end of the bar. Goose and Maverick peered through the haze of colored lights to see cold eyes staring back at them as if they'd been looking a long time and not liking it much. "Tom Kazansky, his name is," Slider added.

Goose was impressed. The Iceman had made himself famous before ever getting there. "No shit. The Iceman," he said. He tipped his beer in the direction of the Iceman. The gesture was rewarded with a curt nod. Iceman was staring at Maverick, like January at the

Pole. He was certainly well named; somebody must have seen his eyes across a barroom and felt the chill. What the hell was he so uptight about? Maverick wondered—but he knew. He knew from previous experience. Somebody was always wanting to prove something. Something about Maverick pissed people off, because something about him signaled right away that he was good, maybe the best, and he knew it. That made some trigger fingers itch to prove themselves faster on the draw. Maybe that was Iceman's problem, maybe not. Maybe Iceman was really that good. Everyone around Top Gun was saying so.

Maverick stood pat, returning the Iceman's stare. Neither one looked away. Then the crowd around the bar shifted and someone moved to block the view. Maverick drank the rest of his beer. He didn't bother looking back that way. He was going to find out for sure who was best before this course was over; he never could resist a showdown.

"Mister-the-Iceman to you," Slider told Goose.

"You think you can get it up five times a day to stay in the sky with us?" Goose asked, looking seriously concerned.

Slider looked at Maverick. "I think, yeah, I think we'll stumble along," he said.

"Oh, this is Maverick. Pete Mitchell. He steers the thing," Goose said.

Slider nodded at Maverick, but still speaking to Goose, he answered, "I hear he steers it pretty close. Sorry to hear about Cougar. He was a good man."

"Still is," Maverick put in strongly.

"Yeah," Slider said. "That's what I meant." He nodded to Goose, then pointedly picked up his beer and went to join Iceman at the end of the bar.

"Shit, Mav—you *saved* Cougar. Looks like the tale got all twisted up crooked, somehow," Goose said.

"Never mind," Maverick answered. "Forget it."

Maverick took a long drink of beer. "Mister Cool, all right," he commented. "Is that why they call him Ice?"

"Nope," Goose said. "It's the way he flies—ice cold. No mistakes. Wears you down, they say. After enough time, you just get bored and frustrated, you do something stupid, and he's got you."

Maverick nodded thoughtfully. He drained the beer and walked away from the bar, into the other room where the music was jumping and so were the customers. The Iceman was sitting with some other fliers at a ringside table. Standing at the edge of the dance floor, Maverick caught a bit of heavy conversation between Wolfman and the lady with whom he was bouncing in time to the music. She was a small, thin girl with painted bright purple fingernails as long as her fingers. They were not so much dancing as gyrating in place and carrying on an intellectual exchange:

"Why do you all have such funny names?"

"The President gives 'em to us," Wolfman answered, snapping his fingers and moving his hips.

She was impressed. She moved closer to him, still bouncing everything that could be bounced. It seemed to encourage Wolfman to explain more. "See, we gotta have a call sign that's just our own, never changes," he explained earnestly. "You have to recognize it immediately. Then, if someone shouts, 'Wolf, break left,' well I just react right away."

"Wolf? Why do they call you Wolf?"

The big bear shrugged, grinning. "Oh, I don't know. Ask the President."

Maverick smiled to himself and moved around the

periphery of the dance floor toward the table where Iceman sat. One of the pilots was droning on and on, shooting down his wristwatch, nobody paying much attention but nobody objecting, either. "We were just really diving down and by then we were right over downtown Haiphong. It was some great shit. Jack says 'What are you doing?' but . . ." Maverick tuned him out and tried to figure a way to engage the Iceman in some small talk.

The Iceman let him stand there a minute or two, and then he glanced up, making almost imperceptible eye contact. He got up from the table and eased off toward the dance floor, Slider right with him. Maverick drank his beer and pondered the Iceman's deliberate rudeness.

Goose sidled by, more or less dancing with a local cutie. He spotted Maverick and boogied closer to report, "Time's a-wasting. You can give me the twenty bucks now."

The girl spoke to Maverick, too. "Is he really married?" she shouted as they shimmied and shook to the beat.

"If he told you he's married, he's married," Maverick assured her. But he was distracted by something wonderful he had either seen or imagined on the other side of the room.

"I knew you weren't married!" The girl laughed at Goose.

It might have been fun to watch Goose's technique for a while, but Maverick's attention was elsewhere. The record ended, the dancing stopped, and in a totally unexpected moment of clarity, Maverick glimpsed the most attractive face he had ever seen.

Chapter 7

DODGING ELBOWS AND snaking around bodies that got in the way of his view, he moved across the room toward her. He saw that she had blond hair that bounced to her shoulder and even in the raw glare of the dance hall lights he could see that there was a shine to it. In another glimpse as he struggled nearer, he saw that she was apparently alone, sitting at a table against the wall and concentrating on something—a book—no, a notebook—on the table in front of her. He got close enough to see that her features were delicate and yet strong, an extraordinary combination he didn't think he'd ever observed before. She was really a beauty. Standing only a few feet away from her, he could see that her hair was a kind of light, spun gold color, and her hands were slender and she wore no rings. She was holding a pen but not writing. Studying, maybe. She looked like she might be a college student.

She was really concentrating, not just pretending to concentrate the way people do sometimes when they're sitting alone in a public place. Just as Maverick decided to engage, a big jock pilot appeared from nowhere and moved in on her. Maverick waited, watching with slowly dawning delight as the jock said something to her, probably asking her to dance, and she looked up, smiled a gorgeous sun-up smile, and shook her head: no, thanks.

This was going to take some maneuvering. Obviously, a head-on approach was not workable. Maverick gulped his beer and went over to Goose, who was taking a breather with Mary Anne while the music got wound up again.

"I'm gonna need some help, brother," Maverick said. He pointed toward the beautiful loner.

Goose frowned. "Which one? That one?"

Maverick nodded. Goose was slightly pissed off. "Aw, come on," he protested. "Have you tried talking to her? Maybe we don't need to do this."

"No, she already waved off one guy." Maverick started walking back toward her. Very reluctantly, Goose turned to his date. "'Scuse me, Mary Anne, I've got to make a fool out of myself. It won't take but a minute." He followed Maverick, leaving Mary Anne to figure it out as best she could.

Maverick went over to the beauty's table. She was still alone, still absorbed in the notebook. He got close enough to see that the page was covered in neatly handwritten columns of calculations. A math major! He loved it. He stood there, noticeably close to her, staring until she had to acknowledge his presence. When she looked up, her gaze was steady and in control. Her eyes were calm and blue as the sky, and she just looked at him, waiting to see what he was up to.

"Oh, no, no, leave her alone," Goose said sternly, coming up to the table like a man in a white jacket with a butterfly net going after the village idiot.

Maverick seemed to be in a trance. He continued to stare until it was pushed into melodrama, a joke. He pointed at her and suddenly sang out, in a surprisingly solid belting voice, a Righteous Brothers love song.

Goose joined in, trying to stop him, "No, no, no . . ." he pleaded. And then he, too, suddenly burst into song.

Most of the people in their vicinity stopped what they were doing and listened to the new Righteous Brothers. Most smiled, some laughed, and some came in closer to dig the action.

Maverick sang, never taking his eyes off what he had now decided was the most beautiful face he had ever seen.

Goose echoed Maverick's vocals plaintively.

Then he paused and turned to the group that was now formed around them. He conducted with both arms; no drunk in the world could resist finishing that song. With full chorus behind them, Goose and Maverick finished with an appalling crescendo.

Everyone applauded cheerfully. The other officers, tipsy or not, appreciated a sharp tactical approach when they saw it, especially if there was a risk, which this seemed to hold. They were rooting for Maverick. Would his maneuver pay off? Twenty guys or more waited for the beauty's reaction.

She looked around and then finally straight at Maverick, and then a melodious laugh that couldn't be held back for another instant poured out like sunshine. The relief in the area was unanimous as she pushed back a chair—hands clapped and empty glasses were raised toward the bar for more. The chorus broke up and went back to their own pursuits. Maverick sat down with a happy sigh. He loved the way she laughed—hard and honestly—and her teeth were as perfect as the rest of her features. Goose gave them both a wave and returned to Mary Anne on the dance floor.

"You are one lucky guy," the beauty told Maverick.

"I hope so," he said, grinning.

"I love that song. God, I have never seen that approach. How long you guys been doing this act?"

He pretended to be thinking, trying to remember. "Since . . . I guess . . ."

"Puberty?"

He grinned. "Yeah, just about then. Little hairs on the face . . ."

She smiled and put her hand out to shake. "I'm Charlotte," she said.

"Maverick."

"Mongrel?"

"Not Mongrel! *Maverick!*"

"Maverick? Did your mother not like you?"

"No, it's my flying name."

"Oh, I see. So you're a flier? Well, I think I shou—"

"A Navy pilot," he interrupted.

She smiled thoughtfully, nodded, and apparently decided not to say whatever she had been going to say. In fact, she seemed to have decided not to talk to him at all. Her full attention returned to the notebook on the table in front of her. After a minute, she started writing. It was some kind of formula, a series of complicated equations he couldn't quite make out. He simply pretended not to notice that she was trying to brush him off. He waited patiently. He was getting to her. She put down the pen and looked up at him again.

"Tell me. Aren't you afraid some girl's going to get embarrassed and run out crying when you do that routine?"

Maverick shook his head cheerfully. "Nah, embarrassment's good for the brain cortex. Keeps blood in the cheeks."

She laughed.

"To tell you the truth," he went on, "we've only done it twice."

He was rewarded by her looking up from the notebook. He got the full benefit of her really knockout eyes. She wore very little makeup, and it was skillfully applied to enhance what she was smart enough to know was already there. The sparkle, for instance, and the deep, ever-changing sky color. Nothing he liked better than blue, that was for sure.

"How did you do?" she asked.

Maverick smiled, remembering. "Crashed and burned on the first one . . ." He trailed off and left it hanging.

"And the second one?" she prompted.

Maverick's big, crooked smile turned his face into an all-American cheerfulburger. His squarish cheekbones and widely spaced eyes gave him an innocent air that sometimes tripped up even people who knew him best. "I'll tell you tomorrow," he said. "But it's looking good so far."

She burst out laughing and so did he. She closed the notebook and put it to one side.

"I'm interested in the language you pilots use," she told him. Maverick was finding himself more and more smitten.

"Ask me anything," he said.

"What's a bogey?"

"Enemy aircraft."

"And six?"

"Six is the rear end of your aircraft. Want another beer?"

"Not yet, thanks. Is it true that you lose consciousness for a few seconds after you take off from a carrier?"

Maverick nodded. "Yeah. Because we get *shot* off, by a catapult. That's why we lose consciousness. The G-force rolls our eyes back and the blood drains out of the brain."

"Sounds like sex," she said.

Maverick rolled his eyes. He was a happy man. "Some sex. *Good* sex," he allowed, thoughtfully.

Charlotte nodded. Then she saw something over his shoulder that changed her mood abruptly. Or maybe she had started to enjoy herself too much, although she seemed too candid and straightforward for that kind of dodging. He was painfully disappointed when she said, "Listen, I really enjoyed talking with you . . . but here comes my friend."

Maverick looked up to see a suit-and-tie, quite a bit older than Charlotte. He had rimless glasses and thinning hair. Maverick wanted to blink and make the bastard disappear, but here he came, moving through the crowd toward them.

"Let me ask you," Charlotte said quickly, "are you a good pilot?"

From the depths of disappointment, hollowly, he answered, "Yeah. I'm okay."

"Good," she said warmly. "Then I won't have to worry about you making a living as a singer."

The older man in the business suit reached their table then, and she introduced him as Perry Siebenthal.

Maverick stood up and shook hands. With one last, lovely smile from Charlotte to go on, Maverick turned and walked toward the bar. He ordered another beer and couldn't resist looking back. Charlotte and Perry Siebenthal were looking over some papers, most intently. Good sign—maybe he was only a business acquaintance. Maverick had never gotten around to asking what her business was, what her notebook contained . . . there were so many things he wanted to know about her. What she wore to sleep on the nights when she was alone . . .

"Figured it out yet?" someone asked, zeroing in directly on Maverick's left ear. He turned to see the Iceman right at his elbow.

"What?" he asked, a little rattled.

The Iceman cracked his face down under his nose where it would have been a smile on anyone else. "Who is the best pilot," he said.

"I know who the best is," Maverick answered.

"Now, I didn't say the luckiest."

Maverick sipped his beer and didn't bother to answer. "Guys fly their whole career without seeing a Mig up close," the Iceman went on. "You are a lucky boy. What do you think it was? Was it the Mig contact that did it? Got you here, I mean."

Maverick looked away, back toward Charlotte. He saw Perry gathering up his papers—maybe he was getting ready to leave.

"Wasn't my old friend Cougar supposed to be here instead of you?" Iceman was going on and on in Maverick's ear.

"Yup," Maverick answered. His attention wasn't really on this conversation, fascinating though it might be.

Charlotte was gathering her things now. He had the enormous pleasure of seeing her glance in his direction, just for a fraction of a microsecond, but glance she did. Then she got up and headed across the floor behind her "friend." It was the first chance Maverick had to see her without a table cutting her in half; her body was as lithe and lovely as her face. She was a knockout, and he saw other eyes turning to appreciate her as she made her way across the room.

"So I guess that means Cougar's the best," Iceman was going on like a dentist drilling in his ear.

"Cougar's good," Maverick agreed. He downed his beer in one massive gulp and strode away. Over his shoulder, he shot back at Iceman, "*I* am the best." He headed after Charlotte.

On the dance floor, bobbing and swaying to the music, Goose was chatting up Mary Anne with a sincerity that could never be taught. "You don't think about death up there, but you think a lot about the danger. One mistake and you're a smoking hole in the ground." On a pause while Mary Anne wrestled with her feelings of awe and sexual response, Goose looked around to see Maverick's beauty walking past. Long legs, great ass—and Maverick a few steps behind her. As Maverick passed him, Goose murmured, "Target passing. Her six is a *ten!* Turn to engage."

"I never knew it was so dangerous," Mary Anne was saying.

Back on his approach, although distracted for a moment, Goose became sincere again. "Oh yeah, danger makes everything down here more meaningful. You feel a certain intensity of life, and you want to grab onto every moment."

Maverick lost sight of Charlotte in the crowd around

the bar. He pushed his way through and out the door. Cars everywhere, parked or moving in and out, people in some of them, doing the same. She was nowhere in sight. But he did catch sight of Perry, the suit-and-tie, at the wheel of a long, shiny Cadillac on its way out of the parking lot. He was alone.

Puzzled, Maverick looked back at the bar as the door swung open. A sign pointed down the hall toward the ladies' room. Without thinking, he followed his hunting instincts and headed for the only bypass she could have taken. He was through the door and inside a small, windowless room before he knew it. There was a chair, an open door leading to a line of sinks and stalls, and a dressing table with the most beautiful mirror in the world, because it was reflecting Charlotte's face. He just stood and looked at her in the mirror, while she looked back, amused.

"Long cruise, was it, sailor?"

She leaned over the dressing table and started to put on lipstick. Her glance strayed, though, to his reflection looking so longingly at her. She laughed easily. "Hold this," she said, tossing him the lipstick. She rummaged in her handbag for another, found it, and began redoing the soft color of her mouth, which kept turning up at the corners. "What did you want to do, just drop down on the tiles and go for it?" she asked.

He answered her seriously. "No. That's not what I had planned."

Charlotte scoffed. "Come on! It isn't?"

"No. Well . . ." Suddenly he grinned. "I thought we could use my coat."

"That does sound lovely," she said, reaching for the lipstick back. He toyed with it, not wanting to part with it because it was something of hers.

"I . . . I came to save you from a big mistake with that older guy," Maverick said.

She laughed again. "And on to a bigger one, with you?"

He nodded. "Yeah, most likely."

"I'm really flattered, Lieutenant, but I think I've done enough damage here tonight. I've got to go to work early in the morning."

"Then what are you doing here?" he asked softly, wanting only to keep her there, no matter what.

There was the sudden intrusion of a toilet flushing, and a large, self-sufficient woman slammed open a door from one of the stalls in the inner room. She came out straightening her skirt, looking for the source of the male voice she was damned near positive she had heard out here.

"Hold on, sucker!" she shouted loudly. "In case you ain't noticed, you are in the *ladies' room.* The question is what are *you* doing here?"

Charlotte tried to keep a straight face. She turned to leave. The other woman was waiting for some kind of answer and was not about to let Maverick off easily. He realized that he was still holding the lipstick and had better think quickly.

"I'm here to talk about a new concept in cosmetics," he said loudly enough so Charlotte might smile one last time, even if he couldn't see it as she walked out the door.

Goose was standing near the door, looking around the bar for Maverick. He spotted the beauty coming out of the ladies' room. She saw him, too, and walked over to say, "Your friend was magnificent." Laughing, she went out into the night, leaving Goose totaled. He stood there with his mouth open, in deep shock. A second later Maverick emerged from the ladies' room.

"God, do I really owe you twenty bucks?" Goose asked him.

Maverick was so intent on watching Charlotte leave that he almost missed the gag. "Nope, you owe me fifty!" he flung back.

Chapter 8

MAVERICK WRAPPED THE G-suit around his waist, sucked in his gut, and zipped up the side. Then, taking a deep breath and holding it, he bent down to zip the leggings up the inseams of his legs. That little operation itself knocked the wind out of some guys in the early days of flight school, but the body learned how to take it and it was probably no worse than Scarlett O'Hara's getting into her corsets, anyway. He stepped into the torso harness, which would act as his parachute harness should the need arise. Then he strapped leg restraints on his calves (they'd be snapped onto fittings on his seat to yank his legs back in case of eject). He shrugged into the survival vest, zipped it, and checked for gear: flare gun, knife, strobe light, water bottle, riser cutters, radio, combination flare and smoke signal. All tucked in neatly, a place for everything and everything in its place. He snapped it together. Helmet in hand, knee-board under his arm, he headed for class.

The hangar was buzzing with movement. Ground crews checking out the planes created their usual hammering and hollering sounds that echoed through the huge space. A little group of pilots and RIOs in full flight suits stood inside Door 4B, facing Jester, who held a clipboard and was concentrating on his watch, counting down seconds until it was time to start the class. At precisely 0500, he started talking.

"In the back of this room stands your enemy," he growled. "Your instructors."

Heads turned to scan the relaxed, poised, and down-and-dirty *mean* faces of a row of men in blue flight suits. Two out of the group wore Top Gun caps. Not a smile in the carload. Jester's voice boomed off the high tin roof and back at the heads that swiveled to attention again.

"Photographs of your instructors are stored in the war room of the Kremlin."

Jester paused so long to let that sink in that some of the fliers started thinking maybe he wasn't kidding. "Let me assure you," he went on, "they fly dirty. You will be trained and evaluated by a few civilian specialists as well. These civilians are here because they are the very best sources of enemy aircraft as well as—"

Footsteps, magnified by the hangar's echo, interrupted the squadron leader's thoughts. He looked up and beyond the line of instructors to greet the newcomer with a huge smile. "Hi, Charlie," he said. The smile disappeared as he turned his attention back to the class. "Okay, good. Our TAGREP is here. Charlie is one of the civilians I mentioned—the one person most qualified to get into P-subs and curves and VN-diagrams. You will pay strict attention to everything Charlie says or you will be real sorry you didn't."

Maverick turned around with the rest of the fliers to get a look at the guy. It wasn't a guy. It was the most beautiful face he had ever seen, and she couldn't hide her slim, beautiful body in that dark blue suit and tailored white shirt, either. The high heels didn't do a thing to hurt the exceptionally wonderful proportions of her legs . . . Charlotte walked past the group down to the front of the room. If her eye caught Maverick's for a millisecond, not even he could be sure of it.

Jester's voice sounded dim, far away, and fading as Charlotte turned to face the class. The color of her eyes was softer in the daylight, and she had the mercy to try to hide them behind big round spectacles that only emphasized the delicacy of her features. Standing next to Maverick, Goose chuckled once, quietly.

He forced himself to look away from her and concentrate on what Jester was saying. "Charlotte Blackwood —code-name Charlie," the leader boomed. The echo magnified the words and bounced them around the hangar like the voice of doom. "Charlie has her Ph.D. in astrophysics. She's a civilian contractor, so you don't salute her, but you'd better listen to her, because the Pentagon listens to her—about your proficiency, among other things. It goes without saying she is to be treated with the best respect your mammy and the Navy ever taught you. Is that clear?"

Hands off, was what he meant. Very clear.

Charlotte—Charlie—started talking in that melodious voice, working hard at keeping it unsexy although, as far as Maverick was concerned, not succeeding.

"Hello," she said. "We will be dealing with F-Fives and A-Fours, as our Mig simulators. Technically, the F-Five does not have the thrust-to-weight ratio of the Mig Twenty-one. It also does not bleed energy below three hundred knots like the Mig Twenty-one does.

The A-Four does not turn as well as the Mig Seventeen but has significantly better visibility. I think I have some new data for you. A Mig Twenty-one has a problem with the inverted flight tanks. It won't do a negative G-pushover."

There was an uncouth snicker from somewhere in the back of the group. Maverick suddenly glimpsed how tough it must be to be a lady—and a gorgeous one, at that—trying to be serious about working with a bunch of jet jocks . . . he was having his own problems, trying to look anywhere but at her, trying to concentrate on what she was saying.

Charlie heard the snicker, hesitated just a flicker of a second, and then went on, unruffled. "The latest intelligence shows that the most they will do in operation is one—is there something wrong, Lieutenant?" She was looking at Goose, who was shrugging his shoulders impatiently.

"I don't think you're altogether right about that," he drawled politely. "The Mig, I mean, ma'am."

"I beg your pardon?" Charlie said. She probably wasn't at all used to being contradicted, but she was interested. Goose ignored the laser-sharp glare Jester was shooting at him. He and Charlie were so interested in their dialogue that they paid no attention when the door opened at the back of the area and Viper walked in to stand alongside the line of instructors behind them.

"Well, no, ma'am, I beg yours," Goose said. "But I don't think you're right on that, about the Mig Twenty-one being able to do a negative G-dive."

"Why not?" Charlie asked. In concentrating on Goose, she was focusing uncomfortably close to Maverick, who wished his RIO would stop making their immediate area so goddamned conspicuous.

"Well, ma'am, we saw one," Goose told her.

"You saw a Mig Twenty-one?"

Maverick couldn't keep on wishing to disappear. This was his experience they were hashing over, and the pilot in him rose above the smitten jerk. "We saw a Mig Twenty-one do a four-G negative dive," he burst out.

She had to look straight at him now, and damned if she didn't take off her glasses and give him both barrels. It wasn't that she was trying to get an unfair advantage. It was just, clearly, that she didn't believe him.

"We?" she repeated.

"Yes, ma'am!" Goose affirmed.

Charlie walked over to them. She was smiling, but there was nothing personal about it. "Where did you see that?" She waited, looking from Goose to Maverick. "Lieutenant?" she said pointedly. Everybody in the room was staring at him and waiting for his answer, and she was standing there smelling faintly of spring lilacs.

He swallowed and hoped his voice wouldn't betray him. He hated to do it to her, but sometimes the only way out of a tight spot was diversionary fire. Or what his mother used to call his sassy tongue that got him into more trouble than it ever got him out of.

"It's classified," he said.

Nervous buzzing from the other fliers. Jester went visibly rigid. Charlie obviously couldn't believe her ears.

"It's what?" she asked.

"Classified," he repeated.

Goose tried to rescue the situation with a bit of a yock. "He could tell you, but then he'd have to kill you," he said.

The vibrating tension in their corner of the cavernous hangar eased up—but only a little. Everyone was aware of the CO's presence, but he was silent, so far.

"Lieutenant," Jester bawled out angrily, "talk to the lady!"

Charlie glanced over her shoulder, back at Jester, stopping him cold. She could handle herself, thank you very much for your trouble, anyway. She was totally collected, didn't need anybody to pull rank on her behalf. It was pretty clear that she didn't want to make it worse for Maverick or deepen his embarrassment, but she was fascinated by the information. An eyewitness who had actually seen the plane that she could only imagine through statistics and blueprints. She spoke calmly, without sarcasm or rancor.

"Lieutenant, I have a top-secret clearance. The Pentagon sees to it that I know more than you."

Maverick nodded politely. "Not in this case," he said, reluctant but honest.

"You saw a Mig Twenty-one push negative four-G?" she asked flatly.

"Yes."

"Where were *you*?"

"On his six."

There was stifled laughter from the men around him.

"He was in a four-G negative dive and you were on his six?" Charlie repeated.

"Yes, ma'am. At first. Then I was directly above him."

She stared at him for a moment. She was awfully

73

pretty. The hangar had gone totally silent except for the drill some mechanic was using far at the other end. She had him now, and, calmly, she went in for the kill.

"If you were directly above him, how did you see him?"

Not even a snicker now—everybody figured the lady had got the better of the smart ass and Maverick was dead in the water. He fidgeted a second or two before he came up with his answer.

"Uh . . . I was inverted."

A laugh that could only have come from the Iceman winged through the room. The other fliers were commenting to each other, this way and that.

Charlie was staring at him as if she'd never seen this particular subspecies before. "You were in a four-G dive with a Mig Twenty-one and you were inverted," she repeated slowly. Obviously, she didn't believe him. *"At what range?"* she asked skeptically.

"Two," Maverick answered.

"Two miles," Charlie said.

"Two meters," Maverick corrected her. He was having trouble looking directly into her eyes because they reminded him of the sky, where he fervently wished he was right now.

Goose couldn't stand the snickering. "One and a half, actually," he piped up. "I took a Polaroid picture."

Charlie diverted her attention to him, but only for a minute. "Would you show it to me?"

"Sure," Goose agreed. "I'll give it to you if you want it. Just a souvenir, to me."

Charlie was staring at Maverick again, as if maybe she could figure him out if she looked hard enough and close enough. The rest of the room was dead silent watching and listening. "Lieutenant," she said finally. "What were you doing there?"

She sure asked all the wrong damned questions. "Uh . . . giving him the bird," he admitted.

There was open laughter at that. Charlie kept on staring at him, not smiling, as if she didn't understand.

"You know," he said uncomfortably. "The finger."

Goose lifted his hand as if to demonstrate, but she turned to him quickly and gracefully lifted her own slim hand, middle finger up. "I know the bird, Goose!" she said.

Laughter pinged off the walls and back. But Charlie wasn't laughing. She was looking at Maverick again. Did he detect a new respect in those deep blue eyes? "So *you're* the one," she said quietly.

Up front, Jester pointedly looked at his watch. "Come on, Charlie," he snapped. "We've got some flying to do this morning."

Eagerly, the men moved out toward the planes. Charlie stopped Maverick with a low murmur. "Lieutenant."

He didn't know whether he wanted to stop or not. He stopped. He pushed a straight lock of hair back off his forehead. He turned and met her gaze.

"You kind of let me make a fool of myself," he said.

"You seemed determined to do that anyway," she answered, not unkindly. "Why didn't you tell me you were the famous Mig insulter?"

"Didn't know I was famous. And when was I supposed to get to that? You didn't seem particularly interested in the story of my life. Anyway, would it have made a difference?" He looked straight at her, really wanting an answer.

She smiled. "Not in the ladies' room."

"What *would?*"

Charlie shook her head, the hint of a smile quickly gone. "Look—I'm assigned to this school. I see sixteen new hotshots every eight weeks. You figure it out. Let's have a cup of coffee—I'd really like to hear about the Mig."

Maverick felt relieved and unbelievably up, all of a sudden. He glanced over at the doors, wide open to the desert sky, where the Tomcats were beginning to roll out. "No," he told her, "I've got to go to work. You've got top security clearance. Maybe you can read about it in a report somewhere."

He walked away. Watching him, she smiled and shook her head. Someone else was watching Maverick, but not smiling at all. Viper had been a silent witness to the whole exchange. Now he stuck his pipe in his mouth thoughtfully and stood in the shadows like an IFF/APX Data Link, taking in all the signals and quietly processing the information.

Chapter 9

GOOSE WAS ALREADY strapped and hooked into the rear cockpit, and the takeoff crew was waiting. Maverick did a walk-around, then let them hoist him up and buckle him down. Lap belt, parachute risers, leg restraints, oxygen mask, G-suit all hooked into support system, communications cord—all in place. He put on his padded skullcap and then the hard hat. Then he armed the ejection seat, rotating the safety lever on the firing handle up and down, doing the same with the alternative firing handle lever behind and over his head. He and Goose went over the preflight checks. All was in order, and Maverick gave the thumbs-up signal to the plane captain, who waved them out onto the flight line.

With the wings still folded at seventy-five degrees storage angle, they taxied to the end of the line and stopped. Maverick lowered the Tomcat's long, pointy nose down for final inspection. Finally, their crew waved them on, and they headed for the runway.

Maverick did the rundown; Goose responded: "Brakes—brakes okay, accumulator pressure up. Fuel

—normal feed, auto trans dumps off, sixteen thousand pounds on the counter, exterior trans checked. Canopy —handle closed, hooks engaged. Seat—all armed forward, all armed rear. Command lever—forward. SAS switches—all on. Circuit breakers—all in. Master test —off. Bidirectional pump—normal. Compass and standby gyro—compass synched, standby gyro set."

Maverick nudged the throttles, engaged the nose-wheel steering, and lined up to the right of the center-line. Ready for final pre-takeoff checks: "Wings— twenty degrees. Visual check—twenty degrees, okay. Flaps and slats down—check. Spoilers—outboard spoiler-mod on. Speed brake, select spoilers up— check. Speed brake off—check. Check trim neutral harness—mine's locked, how about yours? Locked, okay. Check controls—okay. Check warning lights all out, are yours? Mine are—check, all out. Looks like we're ready to fly, Goose."

"Let's go."

They watched over their left shoulders for the signal that their wingman was ready to go. On the "thumbs-up" from the plane captain, Maverick set the brakes, went into Zone Two afterburner, and released the brakes. The F-14 leaped forward. Pushing into Zone Five afterburner gave them both powerful punches to the kidneys: inertia generated by more than 40,000 pounds of thrust from the twin TF-30 engines behind them. They rose at one hundred knots and were airborne after covering less than 1500 feet of runway. Gear and flaps came up. They climbed to 28,000 feet and steadied. Ready for fun and games, they looked around to see who was going to join them on this lovely morning's war games.

The A-5 zoomed into sight only seconds behind them. Jester himself was on the stick. The two planes circled each other, going in opposite directions, almost like a stately eighteenth-century waltz performed at twenty-first-century speed. Jockeying for position, they snapped past each other like the ends of bullwhips. The earth was spinning, the horizon disappearing and reappearing every which way. With each hard turn, Maverick and Goose grunted aloud—life sounds to keep the blood going in the brain so they wouldn't pass out.

The fight was hard, physical, exhausting. Flying a supersonic jet fighter is not like driving a school bus, for all the noise each makes in its own way. Six and a half times the pull of gravity makes your head weigh over a hundred pounds and flattens your body against the seat so that you can't even twitch. It can twist your innards badly if they're not properly strapped up. Every time the plane makes a sharp turn or goes vertical in a soar or a dive—which is what combat maneuvers are all about—your body takes a worse beating than if you were in the ring with the fastest, meanest heavyweight that ever threw a body punch.

Maverick strained to turn his head so he could track the bogey as it streaked past at Mach one.

"I've lost him!" he muttered. "Where is he?"

"On your six," Goose answered crisply, his eye on the Detail Data Display panel in front of him. The DDD showed a blip moving in on them from behind. "Coming hard," he reported. "Four hundred . . . losing airspeed. He's on your six and closing fast! Hard left! *Hard left!*"

Maverick jerked the stick left, and the F-14 took an impossible right-angle turn—there wasn't another aircraft in the world that could do it. Jester tried to emulate but, stuck with an A-5, roared past them into a wide arc.

"Great move. *Great!*" Goose exclaimed.

"I shouldn't have let him get so close," Maverick said.

"Take it down," Goose advised. "Let's bug out of here. Call for a draw."

But Maverick's fighting spirit had been sparked, and it didn't cool down that easily. Up here was control, power, a chance to test himself against gravity and—the leader. Authority. The enemy. Call it whatever you wanted to, he was here to learn combat. "No way," he decided. "I'm going to nail him. Going vertical."

The plane exploded into high afterburner and rocketed toward space. Far below and in direct line with the sun, Jester's canopy was sprayed with a blinding glare. He was ballistic—and going ballistic is dangerous. The plane flies like a bullet, obeying the laws of physics, not the pilot's touch on the instruments. The ballistic aircraft is, for the moment, out of control. The pilot's skill and maneuvering instincts are only as good as his luck, once the plane starts answering to a higher law.

"He's blind—you got him!" Goose exclaimed.

Jester's blare on the UHF was frantic. "No joy! No joy! Where are you? I've lost sight!"

"He's out of energy!" Goose warned Maverick. "You got control? Unload!"

Maverick peeled over in a backward dive. They saw the A-5 rocket down the outside of a wide ellipse— "peeling the egg." This movement gave it renewed power, and within seconds Jester had full control over his plane again. He had lost a lot of altitude. Maverick stayed close enough to keep an eye on Jester's next move, to anticipate, if possible, and take the advantage.

Maverick lined up the A-5 in the diamond in the heads-up display. The tone beeped, high-pitched, right on the mark.

"I've got him!" Maverick grunted.

"We're below the hard deck. Knock it off!" Jester ordered sharply.

"He's right," Goose said over the ICS. "We're at ten thousand."

"No way," Maverick answered, the excitement in his voice rising with the pounding of his fighting blood. "I got you, sucker. You're going down."

Jester maneuvered, but Maverick kept him in the gunsight. The beeping grew louder and faster.

"In the envelope," Maverick shouted. "Fox-two. You're gone, Jester, dead!"

"Roger Fox-two," Jester spat out, confirming the hit from Maverick's Sidewinder missile. There was a hard edge of anger in his voice, barely under control. It wasn't only because he had just been totaled. Jester didn't expect to win them all, flying the A-5 against the F-14, even as an instructor against students. These students were, after all, special . . . no, Jester's fury, under taut control, was due to something else. "Get your butts above the hard deck. Return to base immediately," he barked.

Goose and Maverick were brought up short for a minute, but the thrill of victory got the best of them. Goose let out a war whoop that almost blew the earphones out of Maverick's helmet. The F-14 swept up and rolled into an Immelmann turn.

"We did it!" Maverick shouted.

"Look, Ma, top of the world!" Goose hollered as the

earth careened zanily under and over and around them for a wild, celebratory moment. Then Maverick broke hard and high and started the descent on a distinctly perpendicular slant. Goose watched the world go by sideways for a moment. They were coming in on the landing pattern, but definitely crooked.

"Ahh . . . a little high on the left, don't you think?" he said politely, as if breaking the news that Maverick had forgotten to lift his little finger over his teacup. Nothing serious, just that they were coming in on a wing tip instead of on landing gear.

"Right," said Maverick. He aileron-rolled another quarter turn. Inverted, they passed right down the runway. Goose looked up from his instrument panel and tried not to sweat as the earth went by at 300 knots, upside down.

"Right," he said insouciantly. "Ahhh . . . what do you call this?"

"It's a victory roll," Maverick answered happily.

Goose snorted. "I wouldn't call it victory. It's more like self-abuse," he drawled.

Maverick laughed and showed off just a wee bit more. Still inverted, they zoomed past the control tower at eye level with the old salts inside. One of them, just returning to his post from the coffee machine, spilled the steaming java all down his shirt as they *whooshed* past. Maverick thought that was funny. He took it around again, banking left and waving jauntily as they passed by the observation window one more time.

"Hi . . . hi there," Goose greeted the tower as they flew by. "How y'all doin' in there?" He switched off UHF and back onto the inter-cockpit system. Maverick got a big sigh in his ear. "You know, Mav, at one point I *did* used to want a Navy career."

"Come on, relax," Maverick told him as he completed the roll and banked again. "Now they know who we are."

"You see all those guys with gold on their shoulders?" Goose said. "The one with smoke shooting out of his ears was Johnson, air boss of the *Kitty Hawk*. That's all."

"Come on," Maverick said with a laugh, "we beat an instructor. How many times in your life do you get to do a victory roll?"

"Just once, if they take your plane away," Goose answered philosophically, as they turned into a roll and yaw opposite, five degrees-right wing down and five degrees-left sideslip, heading for touchdown.

Chapter 10

THEY ROLLED OUT, broke over the runway, and came gliding in on the dime. On the flight line, the crew had plenty to say about the victory roll as they helped them unleash themselves. Opinions seemed to be varied as to whether they would get kicked out of school or were automatically shoo-ins for the plaque. Maverick and Goose climbed down and strode down the line toward the barracks.

They passed the Iceman's plane just as he was putting his leg over the step to come down. He had a word for them as they came within earshot: "Cowboys!" He didn't exactly sing it out; it was more like spitting. Maverick kept walking, but Goose hung back. Slider, too, had a comment to make as he got down from the rear cockpit.

"Nice," he said sarcastically. "Always a good idea to show up your instructors." They ignored him, too. As they passed the A-5, just turning into the flight line, they felt Jester's glare shining down on them like cannon shot.

Goose smiled up at the leader. He shrugged eloquently and protested his innocence. "Hey," he said, pointing a thumb toward the rear cockpit out of which he'd just come, "see any controls back there?"

"Hard deck, my ass," Maverick said loudly. "We *beat* the son of a bitch!" He kept on walking, and Goose had to quicken his step to keep up with him.

The locker room was full of a dozen guys getting out of their flight suits. Maverick and Goose came in, carrying their helmets. Everyone looked up expectantly, as they did for all the other students, wanting to know the score. Goose grinned widely and flashed a GO sign with his thumb. This was greeted with "all *right*" and fists raised in victory punches, high fives and hand smacks. The class was forming itself into a competitive but loyal group.

"We won!" Goose burst out.

"Huh?" The general reaction was disbelief, and then chaos.

"You *won?*" Wolfman repeated.

"Didn't everybody?" Maverick asked modestly.

"Ooooo-weeeeee!"

"We got our butts kicked," Wolfman confessed.

"Thirty seconds," Hollywood chimed in. "That's all it took to blow us out of the sky."

Using his hands, big, bearish Wolfman described the action. "We went like this, he went like that. I say to Hollywood: where'd he go? Hollywood says: where'd who go?"

"And he's laughing," Hollywood said grimly. "Right over the radio, he's laughing at us the whole time."

"It was mortifyin'," Wolfman agreed, and the others in the locker room started grousing about their disastrous morning, with open palms and elbows flying in all directions to describe arcs and turns.

The Iceman and Slider strode in. The same expectant hush fell, curves and zooms stopped in midair. Iceman stopped just inside the door, looked around at everyone for a dramatic pause, and then smiled, flashing his thumb up. The men in the locker room whooped and cheered for him as they had done for Maverick and Goose. Iceman handled the attention with the easy composure of one who was used to it.

Maverick busied himself getting out of his G-suit. Goose went over to pound Slider on the back and shake the Iceman's hand. "You won! Congratulations," he said.

"Maverick and Goose won, too," Hollywood told them.

Iceman talked into his open locker, not turning around to anyone, but with the full attention of every man in the room. "That's not what I heard," he said loudly.

"No, hey, no shit, we won!" Goose affirmed.

Iceman turned and stared at Goose for a long, silent moment. Then, with a shrug of dismissal, he bent over to unzip his leggings.

Slider, standing next to him, enlightened them. "Below the hard deck doesn't count. So you did it again—you guys are the alternates, the second team. No points for second place in combat, remember?"

Just as Goose was about to answer, Jester broke into the locker room, snapping orders. "Maverick! Goose! Viper's office. Now!"

In the anteroom outside the CO's office, enlisted yeomen and chiefs were trying to go about their clerical duties, but it was not really possible. They couldn't do anything with that screaming and yelling going on inside. The door seemed to shake with the noise; who'd have thought a human voice could rattle people accustomed to jets taking off and landing? Some of the female personnel seemed acutely embarrassed, although being in the Navy they had to have heard at least some of those words before. Mostly, everyone was out-and-out curious—it wasn't Viper who was doing the yelling; he never did. It was Johnson, the air boss of the *Kitty Hawk,* down for some observing. Why the CO was letting him have his tantrum right there in the office was anybody's guess. One of the yeomen was thinking of taking bets on whether Johnson would bust a gut and have to be carried out.

BOOM! The door burst open—no one had time to start pretending to type or file—or anything. Johnson, huge, hairy, and mean, blasted out as if he were on a catapult. His brawny hulk nearly collided with a slight, brown-haired female petty officer, who almost spilled her tea. Johnson charged like a mad bull toward the door of the anteroom, looking as if he wanted to smash something—anything that got in his way. The clerks instinctively moved aside. He crashed through the door and out into the hall, still muttering loudly and obscenely. The enlisted personnel turned their heads, as if choreographed, toward the CO's office door, which Johnson had left open.

Jester was in there, stone-faced. The two fliers, Maverick and Goose, stood rigid—they were obviously the targets of all this. Viper was standing, too, in front of his desk, no expression on his face. He glanced over and saw them all out in the anteroom, frankly staring. He walked over to the door and grasped the knob. The total lack of expression on Viper's face was scary;

suddenly everyone had something to do—a computer to man, a typewriter, a telephone. Slowly, deliberately, Viper swung his door shut.

The silence inside the office was thick and heavy. Viper still didn't sit down; he leaned his butt on his desk and faced them with his arms crossed. He spoke quietly, like a funeral director consoling the living.

"Well . . . that about covers the flyby."

Maverick and Goose were uncomfortable enough, but when they saw Jester almost breaking into a grin, something shriveled up way down low, inside.

"Now, in addition," Viper went on in that ominously placid, quiet tone, "in addition . . . you broke two major rules of engagement. And . . . that's . . . *not* . . . *good.*"

Maverick and Goose could have been statues. Viper waited a minute and went on. "Lieutenant Candela lost sight of you and called 'no joy.' You failed to respond." Now he waited for an answer.

Maverick frowned slightly and nodded.

"Why?" prompted the CO.

Maverick was exhausted. It had been a long, rough morning. His voice was a hoarse whisper. "I had him in sight. I was coming over the top, into a dive. He saw me when I moved in for the kill. There wasn't any danger—"

Viper interrupted, addressing Goose. "Is that how you remember it?"

"Yes, sir. We had him. By the time we could respond, we were diving right into his view."

Viper was clearly not satisfied with their answers, but he moved on. "The hard deck for this hop was ten thousand feet." Turning to the instructor, he asked in the same, passionless tone, "Jester, at what point did you call off the fight?"

"Just below ten thousand."

Viper looked at Jester for a minute, then said, "But you continued to fight."

Another pause, another grudging nod.

"Why?"

This time Maverick answered. "He knew we had him, sir. We weren't below for more than ten seconds. There was no danger. I had the shot. I took it."

"The rules of engagement are not flexible," Viper said flatly. "They exist for your safety. You *will* obey them. Is that clear?"

For a split second, Maverick thought about continuing the discussion but quickly decided to cut his losses and give Viper what he wanted. "Yes, sir, perfectly clear. I guess we were . . . I was . . . just a little over-enthusiastic."

Viper measured him for a moment. Maverick worried that maybe he had been just on the cusp of *too* sincere. But Viper let it go. "I guess you were," he said. "Dismissed."

When Maverick and Goose had left the room, Viper looked at Jester and then sat down at his desk and picked up Maverick's fitness report. He didn't read it. He just fingered it and looked back up, waiting.

"I don't know what to tell you, Skip," Jester said. "He's the seat of the pants . . . completely unpredictable. Nothing by the book. All over the sky."

Viper allowed himself a crooked half-smile. "He got you, didn't he?"

Jester nodded, and the CO laughed. "Maverick!" he exclaimed, throwing the report back on the desk.

"Means a wild pony," Jester said.

"You know whose kid he is?" Viper asked him.

Jester nodded. "Yeah. I don't think I've ever heard the whole story on that, though."

"Tell me one thing," the commanding officer asked thoughtfully. "If you had to go into combat, would you want him with you?"

Jester turned and walked slowly around the room. The walls were lined with photographs—planes and pilots—and plaques and commemorations and letters from three Presidents about the glories of Naval aviation. Jester paced and pondered. Finally he replied.

"Yes."

Viper snapped shut the fitness report.

After every flight, a jet jockey needs to move his body. Wearing all those pounds of gear and spending tense time strapped into an area the size of your cat's bathtub makes workout time a necessity. Maverick headed straight from Viper's office to the gym.

After forty chest-pulls on the machine, he was soaked in sweat and exhausted, but feeling much better. He stopped to rest, and Tombstone, the instructor, threw him a towel. Maverick wiped his face and arms, thinking about a good hot sauna and a cold shower and sleep . . . and the Iceman slid into the twin machine right next to him.

Maverick didn't even stop to think. Throwing the towel back to Tombstone, he began to pull again. He had a good rhythm going by the time Iceman got himself settled, but Iceman quickly picked it up and they were like a pair of Radio City Rockettes going at it in perfect tandem.

Maverick wouldn't quit. Neither would Iceman.

Sweat began to pour like the June thaw off the Rockies, but both machines kept up the steady, inexorable rhythm as muscles popped and strained; the contest went on and on until Maverick thought he would burst. His face was contorted; grunts and groans couldn't be held back, but he kept pulling and pulling and—suddenly—there was no more strength, nothing to pull with at all. He was finished. He dropped down hard. The padded table was soaked with his sweat. He looked over at the other machine. It was empty. Iceman had gone.

Tombstone winked at him and threw him a dry towel. The trainer sat down on the empty table.

"You okay?" he asked.

Maverick nodded. "Listen, there's stuff I want to know," he said, gasping to get his breath back.

"About him?" Tombstone indicated the departed Iceman with a shrug of his head. "Well, he's—"

Maverick shook his head. "Not Iceman. I mean Viper."

Tombstone looked only mildly surprised. He collected his thoughts and spoke slowly and deliberately. "Viper? The man is death . . . the Prince of Darkness," he said ominously. "He's got no flaws. He was born to be a flying weapon. He's a Mig killer, but almost everything he's done is classified. No one knows much about anything, except that he is . . . Mister Death."

Maverick listened carefully. "Will he fly against us?" he asked.

"Rarely," Tombstone told him. "Maybe against the Top Gun."

Maverick threw down the towel. "I'd be proud to fly against him," he said seriously.

Tombstone picked up the towel, stared at Maverick, and then shook his head. "You'd better cool down," he said laconically.

Maverick stood in the shower a long time, making promises to himself. And he always kept his promises, especially the ones to himself.

Chapter 11

MAVERICK AND GOOSE sat at a table behind Iceman and Slider. They were in the library, forcing their minds to concentrate on the physics of what they did up there in the air. It was always tough—forcing yourself to do on paper what you could do instinctively in a jet without all those pages of calculations. Sometimes you just couldn't get it to come out right in a notebook—but you *knew* that, behind the controls, when things were real, everything would snap into place. Today, paperwork was even tougher than usual for Maverick—Charlie was monitoring the study session. He couldn't keep his eyes on the books, charts and maps spread out on the table. His eyes kept drifting around the library, feigning casualness, but always coming to rest, if just for a moment, on that wonderful-looking instructor.

Finally, Charlie got up from her chair, smoothed her skirt, and, carrying a clipboard, moved slowly down the aisle. She stopped next to Maverick.

"Here's your simulator evaluation," she said, looking Maverick in the eye and handing him a piece of paper.

Maverick just nodded and began to read her comments. "Okay, lieutenant," Charlie finally said quietly, "I'm sorry."

Maverick simply sat there for a long moment, looking at Charlie. She, too, kept her gaze on him, and at last broke the silence. "Let me put it another way," she said slowly. "You deserved it . . . but . . ."

"I know," Maverick said confidently. He broke out into a broad smile.

"You know what?"

"That you were tempted. You want to go to dinner?" Maverick shot back.

Smiling because she had anticipated him, Charlie wound up the conversation brightly. "No, thanks. I never date students."

Mimicking a man who has just been shot with a particularly sharp arrow, Maverick clutched his heart and reeled back in his chair. He was grinning. She threw a little smile in his direction and turned to walk away.

"Just a second," Maverick called out to stop her going. "What's the co-efficient for this?" he continued, pointing to the worksheet in front of him.

Charlie turned and came back to Maverick's side. She leaned over the desk, a lock of hair falling over her cheek to obscure his view of her. She thought for a moment and then said, "Try this one here," as one long slender finger pointed to the top of a page.

"Was I too fast?" Maverick asked, mock-innocent.

Charlie pushed the hair out of her face and looked at him. "Maybe," she said, "Maybe too aggressive."

"Yeah," he agreed. "When I see it, I go after it."

Maverick was smiling, but he suddenly became serious. "Look, if the government trusts me, maybe you could too?"

Charlie looked at him steadily; she'd never seen Maverick being serious before. She started scribbling something on her clipboard. As she wrote, she said, with a half-smile, "It takes more than just fancy flying." Charlie tore a scrap of paper from the sheaf on her clipboard and handed it to Maverick. Then, not turning back again, she strode down the aisle and left the library. Maverick didn't take his eyes off her until the door had eased shut and she was gone. Then he looked at the paper she'd handed him. It read:

503 Laurel Beach Road
5:30
Be on time!

Maverick touched his forehead in a kind of salute, sort of a very happy see-you-later. He was still smiling as he left the library and turned down the hall past the computer analysis room.

Five o'clock found him combing his hair and reviewing calculus from a volume propped up against his mirror; he hummed along with the radio and half-listened to the shouts and insults beating up to his window from a fierce volleyball game outside. He was wearing jeans and a polo shirt—casual. He was trying to stay cool as he closed the book, turned the radio off, and started to leave his room.

"Maverick!" It was Goose, out in the hall but coming hard in his direction. Maverick tried outmaneuvering him but underestimated the mountain man's raw speed. Goose saw him and shouted again. Maverick stopped and turned around, enduring his RIO's close inspection.

"Free time, man," Goose said, deciding not to comment on the hairdo, the clean polo shirt, the air of a man on his way to something special. "Come on, our honor has been besmirched."

"I got to study, Goose."

"Well, where, man? All dressed up and all?"

Maverick had been leading the way down the corridor to the outside door. The volleyball game had temporarily suspended play, but insults were still wafting across the early evening from the other side of the building. With Goose still dogging his tail, Maverick reached the parking area and headed for his motorbike.

"Tomorrow, Goose," he said.

"Sure. Leave me to deal with *your* honor." Goose stood there like a forlorn lamb, tall and gangly but lonesome and blue. It could have been pathetic if you didn't know Goose. Maverick threw a leg over his bike.

". . . challenge from Slider . . . and Iceman—"

Maverick didn't throw his switch. He sat there just for a minute.

". . . saying you are a chicken shit . . ."

Maverick's leg came back down off the bike. He stood there staring at Goose. Was this for real?

". . . that it runs in your family."

The game was vicious. It was just Maverick and Goose against Slider and Ice, a tough match that was, of course, a lot more than a game. The other players had backed off, preferring to spectate this one, and it was two-on-two, with the ball taking a hell of a beating. Slider and Goose were facing off on either side of the net, each clearly trying to spike the ball right smash into the other's face; friends they may have been, and would be again perhaps, but there had been some meanness building up and this was where it all came out. Sounds of punching and slapping and grunts and "ughs" as the meanness flowed into the game and out. Iceman and Slider won the first round. Slider and Goose walked away from the net, together. They fell to the grass and waited with the other onlookers for the playoff.

The Iceman took off his shirt. He was broad and tanned and had a fair amount of hair on his chest. Maverick took off his shirt, too. Now it was one-on-one. Iceman smashed, Maverick returned a speedball, fast and low and accurate. Iceman spun it back with his fist—Maverick had to duck it but managed to punch it up high and over. It came back, fast, and was slammed down again. Over and over—and then Iceman faulted. The ball rolled off on his side. He raised his foot furiously to kick, but instead he scooped it up and spun around to face the net again, ready for another chance.

The light was beginning to fade. It had to be past 5:30 already. Maverick shook his head, put his polo shirt on over a very sweaty torso, and headed for his bike.

The little house on the beach was in a line with other little houses, with enough space between so that you could walk to the water anywhere along there. It was quiet and dark. He rapped on the door and waited. No answer. He rapped again. And again.

He walked around to a window and peered in. A little table had been set for two, and there were fresh flowers in a bowl. Next to the table, on a counter between the kitchen and the other room, a serving platter was covered with foil wrap. Maverick walked around to the back of the house. There was a wide deck, facing the beach. He looked up and down but saw no one. He walked back to the street, got on his bike, and started it up.

Maverick rode between the houses to the wide sand and started exploring the beach, first in one direction, then after a while he turned around and rode back to the house, past it in the other direction. No Charlie.

Disconsolate, pissed off at himself, he came back to her house, but instead of heading back to the street, he cut his engine just to sit there for a minute or two. How in the hell was he going to fix this one—why did he always manage to fuck up one way or another? But there was always a way out for him, and—he smelled something in the air. STEAKS! Steaks broiling on charcoal and hickory chips . . . and he heard music, too. Maverick's uncharacteristic moment vanished into the abyss where self-doubt belongs—forgotten. He smiled happily and parked the bike.

Charlie was refixing the dinner when he appeared in the open doorway. She didn't look up, but she was relaxed, not angry at all.

"No singing, Lieutenant," she said, smiling at the salad she was tossing.

He laughed. "I'm—"

"And no apologies, Lieutenant," she said easily. "Sit down."

Instead, he looked around the little house. He wandered into a hallway off the living room, through an open door into her study. It had two computers in it. Charts of aircraft covered the walls—high tech. But there were flowers everywhere, too. He came back into the kitchen. She was just outside the screen door, turning the steaks on the charcoal grill.

"Could I take a shower?" he asked her.

Charlie was taken by surprise on that one—even shocked. She looked at him. He looked okay. Then she laughed that marvelous freshwater laugh of hers, and he knew for sure it was really okay. "Hell no," she said. "I'm hungry."

Chapter 12

DINNER WAS SIMPLE, but care had been taken. Everything was finely detailed and delicious—carved little carrots, bread that someone had baked that day, arugula and fresh dill in the salad, just the right amount of tang in the dressing, steaks charred on the outside, pink and thick and juicy when cut into. He was overwhelmed. But the best part was that Charlie enjoyed it as much as he did—more—and wasn't coy about saying so. She wasn't the least bit uptight about his having been late, either.

"Great carrots, Charlie! I love them this way," she said as she helped herself to thirds.

But Maverick was not entirely at ease. Ordinarily he could bull through any situation, but he liked her more and more, and he had let that damned, stupid volleyball game stand her up for over an hour. It was starting to be important to him to be forgiven for that. She was an honest lady; he respected that and wanted her respect back. All this was very new and strange to him.

"Please let me apologize," he said quietly.

Charlie laughed. "No way!" she said. "It's like putting a muzzle on a man if he can't apologize for being late. A lady's got him. And *she* gets to talk. Besides, your being late gave me time to think."

He just loved this woman, she was wonderful. He ate and stared and listened as she went on thoughtfully. "I rent my house. I lease my car. I have a cat, but he's a stray I found on the beach. I get my regular mail at a post office box in Bethesda, Maryland, because I move around a lot. I'm trying for a major promotion, and if I work hard as hell I won't be here much longer." She paused and took a bite of steak and then said, "I've probably got twenty IQ points on you, and yet—you are the first student pilot I've ever let *near* this place. And all in all, I was . . . perplexed about that."

She was falling for him. He could hardly believe it, but he believed it. It was the closest thing to flying, looking at her, eating this dinner, and listening to the music of what she was saying.

"But then I figured it out. Right there in front of me. I thought—he's a smart guy. I'll just tell him why I've got him here."

He stopped eating and looked at her. "Why?"

"It's the Mig," she said.

Maverick had been shot down. And with a mouthful of food.

"The Mig!" he repeated dumbly.

She leaned toward him, more animated than he had ever seen her, and she forgot about food as she explained. "You're the only pilot I've ever talked to who has been up against that new machine. In my business, whole careers are made over great analyses of a new weapon like that Mig Twenty-one. If I can get something—anything—new about it, it'll help me do a better job. If I do a better job, I'll *get* a better job."

Maverick chewed and swallowed and listened carefully. Okay, so it was going to be a chess game. She had made the opening move. Good. He liked games just fine. This was going to be more interesting than he thought. He smiled at her and nodded. "That's it?" he asked. "Got it all figured out?"

She nodded.

"Then where is the wine?" he asked in the same tone of voice.

"Wine?" He had her off guard. She actually looked confused for a second. Then she jumped up. "Oh, my God. I forgot the wine." Check.

She brought a chilled bottle of Chablis from the fridge and filled both glasses. His move.

"You got any Bill Evans music?" he asked. He took a long, cool sip. It was dry, of course, light and delicious.

"How did you know? Yes." She went to put the record player on.

"Do you always get what you want?" he asked her, admiring the way her jeans fit her long, slim legs as she leaned over to start up the record.

She didn't look up. "Well . . . not alwa—yes," she admitted.

"Well, then, relax about the Mig," he told her. He got up from the table and went over to sit on the couch. She sat down on the other end of it, cautiously. Maverick leaned back and closed his eyes, listening to the music. He was aware of her watching him. It was okay. It was more than okay.

"My mother loved this stuff," he murmured. "Used to sit alone for hours and listen to it."

"Why? She was alone a lot?"

Maverick opened his eyes. "I figured with your security clearance, you'd know more about my father than I do."

"Didn't get that far," Charlie told him.

He reached into his pocket and took out the Navy Cross. He tossed it the few inches over to her, and she made a neat catch. She looked at it and then up at him, quizzically, cradling the cross in her palm.

"Big mystery," Maverick told her. "He disappeared. In an F-Fourteen. They wouldn't even say where. I guess someplace he shouldn't have been. The smell of it was that he screwed up." He couldn't help feeling the anger again, rising in his throat. "No way! He was a great pilot." Maverick made his voice calm down again. "But who the hell knows? It's all classified."

"Somebody must know," Charlie said softly.

Maverick nodded. "*Somebody* knows everything," he agreed bitterly.

Charlie veered the subject a little. "Well, there's something *I* don't know. I don't know why you are always second best up there."

A direct hit. Maverick just stared at her, stunned. Her voice was gentle but professional again. "This is no bullshit," she said. "I have *never* seen anyone fly like that in the simulator. Why are you always second on the list?"

"Well, you are direct, aren't you?" Maverick said uncomfortably. But she made him think hard about something he'd been avoiding thinking about. She waited while he sorted it out, and she listened carefully when he finally started talking. "I've got no money. Didn't go to Annapolis. All I've got is my instincts. They don't always salute exactly when the parade goes by. I fly like I fly . . . because I . . ." He trailed off, his thoughts a jumble.

". . . don't know any better?" she offered.

Maverick looked at her. She was very, very beautiful, but—"God," he said, "I don't know if I like you or not."

Charlie didn't smile. "Look, I talk like you fly," she said. "If I see it, I say it. Got that from my Norwegian granddad. Here's how I see it: you and I are both too good to piss away our lives being second best."

Maverick rolled his wine around the tall-stemmed glass. He thought hard about what was going on here. It didn't bother him that she was so close. It bothered him that she was right. "Okay," he said. "What am I gonna do for you?" He looked up from the wineglass, meeting her disturbing eyes like a head-on collision.

She was suddenly flustered, but she overcame it quickly. "You're going to tell me about your Mig."

His instincts were still good. There was something else happening; she felt it, too. He kept looking at her and said, "I'm sorry for being late."

"Well . . . I'm sorry for being too direct," she said. Maverick leaned closer to her and reached for her hand. He took the Navy Cross back from her. Then he put one finger on her lips, which were fine and tempting.

"No apologies," he reminded her.

So softly that it was almost a whisper, Charlie said, "Look . . . this is complicated for me."

He eased away with an understanding smile. He stood up.

"Where are you going?"

He half turned back to her. "I'm going to take a shower," he said over his shoulder.

She watched him apprehensively. But he wasn't heading for the hallway leading to her bedroom; he went to the front door, instead. "Thanks," he said honestly. "I like being here."

He left. He thought maybe it was a draw at that point, having no way of knowing that back inside the house, at the sound of his bike revving up, Charlie lay down on the couch with a seriously disappointed sigh.

Chapter 13

THE TACTS RANGE is an area of the desert completely enveloped by computerized radar. The computers calculate the positions and velocities of a number of planes, by means of transponders in the aircraft and ground stations that talk to each other thousands of times per second. Using this system, it is possible to track aerial combat instantaneously, to give pilots directions, and also to play back the combats for analysis.

In a trailer strategically parked among the complex of antennae, five-foot-high double viewing screens faced the peanut gallery—rows of straight chairs set facing the screens. Student pilots and instructors sat studying the action as the CO explained and queried and ran the show.

State-of-the-art computer graphics duplicated the 3-D view of jets streaming across the screen from various angles. Flight data was displayed as well. In the back of the trailer, computer operators pushed buttons to punch up different points of view of the battle: from the pilot seat, from the RIO's rear cockpit, a long-range angle showing the topography of the landscape and the height of the mountains, and an overhead view of the plane wherever it snaked and streaked—God's point of view.

"The bandit has good position right here," Viper was saying. "All right, freeze the frame. The moment of choice—the F-Fourteen is defensive. He has a chance to bug out right here . . . better to retire and save your plane than force a bad position."

The door to the trailer opened, momentarily flooding the room with sunlight. A slim form slipped inside and took a seat. "Jump in here anytime, Charlie," the CO said.

She studied the screen and nodded.

"Stay in the diamond another three seconds," Viper went on, "and the bandit will blow you out of the sky. Make a hard right, select Zone five—that way, you can extend and escape. But you make a *bad choice*. Comments?"

The film of the day's combat resumed. Almost immediately, Charlie spoke up. "The F-Fourteen performs a split *S*? That's the last thing you should do. The Mig is right on your tail . . . freeze, there. Look, the Mig has you in his gunsight. What were you thinking, there?"

She looked around the room for the pilot. She had come in late. She had no way of knowing who was being evaluated.

"I *wasn't* thinking," Maverick said after a minute. "I just did it."

Chagrined, but with full speed ahead, Charlie went on. "Big gamble with a thirty million dollar plane, Lieutenant."

Maverick smiled cockily. "No guts, no glory."

Some of the students laughed, and there was even a whistle in appreciation for his nerve. Someone gave Maverick the high sign.

"Your guts," Charlie said shortly. "His glory."

Maverick slumped down in his chair. The computer rendering rolled forward again. He glanced sideways at her; Charlie shot him a fraction of a glance, which said: "I told you it was going to be complicated!"

Viper had the floor again. "Unfortunately," he said, "the gamble worked, or you might have learned something. The Mig never got a clean shot . . . Maverick made an aggressive vertical move here, he comes over the top and defeats the bandit with a missile shot. The encounter was a victory, but we've shown it as an example of what *not* to do. I hope you all get the message. It was foolhardy, unthought-out, and he got away with it by luck only. Next reading."

While the computer was loading the next case, Hollywood leaned over to Maverick and whispered, "Gutsiest move I ever saw." Maverick nodded his appreciation, but his eyes were on the back of Charlie's bouncy golden hair.

A different plane and different set of readout statistics came up on the screen. "This is Iceman," Viper announced. "Okay, look at this. It's textbook. Ice takes control of the battle immediately. He never gives the bandit a chance to take the offensive. An early turn here—excellent. He goes for the jugular, and it's over just that quick."

"Let's run that again. It's exactly how it should be done." Charlie's voice was cold, her words loathsome. She fixed him with an ultra-professional stare. Not a trace of the warmth of their private meeting remained. Charlie opened that beautiful mouth to say something else. But Maverick didn't stay for it. He spun out of his seat, out of the room, and out of the building. Slamming doors as he went, he furiously tried to understand Charlie. Why had she critized him that way? In front of everyone. Couldn't she have cut him a little slack—or at least said nothing at all? Maverick's jaw was set in a hard line. He didn't need to take it—not from anyone, but especially not from her. In the sunlight, he squinted and reached for his sunglasses. At the end of the building, the chrome on his bike glinted. It was made for speed. And so was he. In one smooth movement, he straddled the bike and began to rev up, each rev more furious than the last. When he had it humming, he saw Charlie out of the corner of his eye. She was walking fast—not running, but almost—toward him. Maverick gunned the engine again, and settled himself on the seat.

Charlie was now next to the bike. "I . . ." she began, but was cut off by another gunning of the engine. She moved from foot to foot, leaned toward him, and tried again, "Maverick . . ." Again, he cut her off, pointing a finger toward his ear to indicate he couldn't hear her above the din of the racing engine.

Charlie tossed her head in anger. "LIEUTENANT! My review of your flight performance in the TACTS was right on target in my professional opinion!"

Maverick kept looking at the bike's console. "I can't hear you," he said calmly when she'd finished. Then, deliberately, he backed out of his parking space, spun the machine around and headed out onto the street with a roar of noise and speed.

For a second, Charlie watched him leave. Then, determined, she spun on her heel and ran through the lot.

Maverick was satisfying his need for speed. His hair whipped by the wind, he zoomed out of the base. In front of Miramar Gate, he glanced in the rearview mirror. Behind him, closing in fast, was a black convertible, a Porsche. Charlie was in the driver's seat.

Maverick took the turn out of the base at high speed. Charlie's Porsche was close behind him, her hair whipping around her face as she accelerated. Maverick turned the bike steadily and weaved past a slow-moving sedan; she followed suit.

The motorcycle approached a light just as it was turning yellow. Revving, he wheeled his way through. But the Porsche missed the light; now it was solidly red. With her own flash of speed, Charlie whipped through the light and into the intersection. Two cars, one coming from her left and one from her right, narrowly avoided missing her and each other. But Charlie did not pause or look back. She pressed on through the intersection, never letting Maverick's bike out of her sight.

Slowing now, Maverick shook his head, He turned the bike toward the curb, about a block beyond the intersection. Charlie, with a slamming of the brakes and a skid, pulled up behind him. Maverick, pulling off his sunglasses, swung off the bike. With cars whipping past her, Charlie jumped out of her car and plunged toward him.

"You're more afraid of this than I am," she said aggressively, swinging her hair out of her eyes.

"What the hell are you doing?" Maverick shot back, equally tense.

"I'm going to finish my sentence, Lieutenant. My review of your flight performance was right on target . . ." She paused. "But I held something back."

Maverick loosened his stance a bit, and looked at her, telling her with his eyes that he wouldn't interrupt.

Charlie took a breath, but her face was still set in hard lines. "I saw some real genius in your flying, Maverick. But I couldn't say that in there. I was afraid . . ." Her face softened a bit. "Everyone in that TACTS review would've seen right through me. I . . . just didn't want anyone to know . . . I'd fallen for you."

Maverick's face was wide-eyed. He looked shocked.

Charlie continued, "Now I see you've got the same problem."

Finally, she was silent. Slowly, tension in the air, they began to move toward each other. Charlie lifted up long arms and put them around Maverick's neck. They looked at each other for what seemed like forever. Then, inexorably, they moved into each other and kissed.

Somehow, they found their way to Charlie's house on Laurel and into the bedroom. The light had faded, and as they undressed, their bodies made shadows on the darkening window. They kissed, hard and for a long time. Standing up, leaning toward each other harder and harder, their kisses became more and more passionate, more and more breathless. Charlie finally backed off an inch or two and looked at Maverick.

She spoke softly, word by word: "I really don't want anyone on the base to know about us."

Maverick smiled. "My lips are seal—"

That kiss was another long, deep prelude. Charlie let

herself lean fully into Maverick's arms. He held her, stroking her back. The kisses began to be hungrier and hungrier; they stood and kissed and felt their bodies against each other until they gently swayed back and forth, as one silhouette against the window. By the time they managed to release each other long enough to move to Charlie's bed, it was pitch black outside.

Bright sunlight woke Charlie up. She let herself open her eyes slowly, waiting for her senses to fill. She looked across her bedroom and listened carefully for noise, maybe of the shower. The house was quiet; Maverick was already gone. Lifting her head a little, Charlie looked over at his pillow. It was perfectly plumped up, and perched on the top lay a fresh flower and a piece of white paper expertly folded into an F-14. Slowly, Charlie reached for the plane and examined it from all sides. Idly, she unfolded it. Reading the note that was scribbled inside, she hugged her knees to her chest and smiled.

══ Chapter 14 ══

HOLLYWOOD AND MAVERICK flew perfect formation, streaking like twin comets across the sky, faster than sound, with coordination so keen that they seemed two parts of one intelligence. Nature devised ways for flying creatures to sense each other's next move; this adventure was devised by man, and the sensations were like nothing ever imagined by the earthbound.

They banked left, smoothly but with a wrench to the gut—G-suits squeezing at closing up on three times the force of gravity. The horizon tilted to ninety degrees and Maverick pulled around to the right, following Hollywood's lead like Ginger Rogers taking cues from Fred Astaire. A hard bank left—the Tomcat did this better than any plane yet invented. They could feel the power, the limitless freedom to do almost any damn thing at all with this aircraft. The unique air-control maneuvering capabilities of the F-Fourteen, techno-light-years ahead of anything else in the air, twin afterburning turbofan engines, swinging wings automatically positioned by the Mach Sweep Programmer, maneuvering flaps that allowed more G to be applied right from the pilot's stick, the leading edge maneuvering slats that could be preprogrammed for automatic deployment—the F-Fourteen flew like a goddamned bird, only better. Faster and able to do turns that would croak any God-made creature foolish enough to try. Of course, birds didn't try to destroy each other in the air on a regular basis . . . the AWG-9 radar and the "magic" weapons system were two more reasons why the Tomcat beat anything else going. It could carry several variations of Phoenix, Sidewinder, and Sparrow missiles, not to mention the M-51 or M-61 cannons. Fast and lethal—two attributes God hadn't felt the need to give His flying creatures.

"Two at seven o'clock, Jester. Scramble." The voice came as a surprise, and from nowhere, over the UHF plane-to-plane radio.

"Roger, coming left," came Jester's reply.

"Holy shit, that's Viper," Goose muttered into the inter-cockpit mike. "Viper's up here." Then they saw them—two bogeys flying side by side at five thousand, outlined by the blue Pacific ocean. F-5s coming to get them, their instructor and the CO at the controls. They were tiny specks at first, seemingly suspended between the pale sky and the deeper azure expanse of sea below and looking harmless. But quickly enough they would become stinging, deadly fighters, enemies to be dealt with. "Viper!" Goose repeated.

"Great!" Maverick replied. "He's probably saying, 'Holy shit! It's Maverick and Goose!'"

"Sure," Goose managed to gulp before the action was on them. The bogeys split. Bogey One took a hard left swoop; Bogey Two went hard right. Without a second's hesitation, Hollywood swept left in pursuit of Bogey One. Maverick hung back to cover, with an eye on his own tail. He didn't go after the second bogey, sticking close to the rules of battle. It was his job to cover Hollywood, and he circled the action, diving and ascending to keep all three planes in his sights.

Bogey One made a strong vertical move, straight up into the glaring sun; Hollywood stayed on him. Maverick scanned the area, watching out for Hollywood while Goose took care of keeping an eye on Bogey Two.

"Stay with him, Wood—your six clear!" Maverick reported.

Bogey One looped and came down fast. Hollywood almost lost him for a minute, then straightened out and regained the angle. "Stay with him! Tighten your turns!" Maverick warned him.

"Bogey at three o'clock high! Nose on!" Goose reported suddenly.

Maverick flicked his glance starboard and up—Bogey Two was back, ready to pick a fight with him. He jerked the stick to the right. The two planes made a quick pass.

"Snapshot . . . missed him!" came Viper's emotionless voice.

Maverick made a fast decision. "Engaging the other guy, Wood. You're on your own."

Goose groaned loudly. "Just cover Wood, Maverick," he protested. "Mutual support, man!"

"I'm gonna take him, Goose."

Goose was disgusted and within the private confines of their cockpit-to-cockpit hookup, he didn't mind saying so. "Don't be greedy. Stay with Wood."

"I want Viper!" Maverick shot back. As he said it, he grasped the stick hard and took the plane straight up into a vertical climb.

"Hey, come on—hey!" Goose rarely got angry, but his drawl had turned into a growl this time. Fun and games were one thing; being a show-off and a—well, a maverick—could go for a while, but it was growing a little late to get away with kid tricks anymore. He was really pissed off. Maverick was hell-bent on ruining both of them—their careers, if not their lives. It occurred to Goose that Maverick took chances that weren't jokes, anymore. There was something going on, and whatever happened, he was, willing or not, a passenger. Was Maverick trying to self-destruct? It was down-and-out scary, all of a sudden. And Carole was coming, with their baby boy, this very night. Shit. He wanted to be able to tell her everything was going great . . . and here they were, fucking up again.

The thing was, you didn't have to fly with anyone you didn't feel totally good about. It wasn't good business for the Navy to send up teams who didn't trust each other, so if either one of the pair of fliers on an F-14 wanted to change partners, the brass asked no questions beyond what you wanted to answer—they just made the switch. You flew with someone you trusted with your life, that was the way it was. And the fact was that Goose knew Maverick and was proud as hell to fly with him. Maverick was the best pilot in the Navy, very likely in the world. And Goose should know—wasn't *he* the best damned RIO?

Maverick looped down to get an angle over Viper. Not happy with the position, Viper took off, eluding him, running from the fight. Off to their starboard, Hollywood was still flying a vantage position over

Bogey One. "Hang on," Maverick muttered. He took a hard right, streaking after Viper.

"What are you doing? We're cover!" Goose yelled.

"Wood's okay. I want *him.*"

"But we're *cover!*"

It was as if something had got hold of Maverick, some crazy compulsion, an obsession that didn't respond to rational argument. Goose said a silent goodbye to the hope of achieving Top Gun and a stable family life. But something of the excitement of the chase got into his blood, too. In a minute, he too had forgotten that this was an exercise, with rules to be followed. They were engaged in a life-death fight with enemy aircraft. This was what it was all about, and they were on top! They were in charge up here, he and Maverick. They owned the sky and they were the best damned team in the universe. Getting the Bogey was all that mattered. Getting him before he got them. Go for it!

Bogey Two cut trails in the sky, but Maverick stayed close on his tail. He pushed the throttle forward to Zone 5—full afterburner. Viper showed every trick he could pull out of the F-5: hard right, then hard left, rolling into vertical, flapping into a dive. Maverick stayed with him.

Turning to get Viper in the diamond, Maverick heard the growl of a Sidewinder in his headset. "What's the range, Goose?" he asked. "I've got a good tone."

Viper rolled and flipped, but Maverick stayed with him. Viper's plane showed up in the diamond—they had him in their sights. The tone went crazy. But suddenly Goose was shouting urgently: "Two bogeys! Three o'clock high, nine o'clock high! Break!"

They came out of nowhere, flashing down toward

them—a cross-fire ambush. Maverick was startled. His eyes opened wide and he realized instantly there was nowhere for him to go. Viper got out of his diamond and his voice came calmly over the UHF band: *"Atoll* zeroed in on the northern F-Fourteen. He's out of the fight."

Out of the fight. Maverick had been tricked, humiliated. He was stunned. Viper poured a little salt in the wound: "Walked right into it. Not only that, but Zorro got your wingman while your back was turned. Nice going, Maverick."

Goose found his voice. "The Defense Department regrets to inform you that your sons are dead because they were *stupid*. Great balls of fire!"

"Both dead, only one stupid. Sorry, Goose."

"Knock off the chatter, Top Guns. Let's R.T.S. Viper has the lead." The battle was over. Time to go home and get scalded down. For a split second, Maverick found himself wishing that it had been a real battle, that the question of the near future didn't have to be faced at all. Then he had to smile ruefully at himself, behind his mask where no one could see it. He turned to follow the leader in nice military formation all the way home.

In the locker room a half hour later, Goose couldn't seem to lose his hangdog expression. Maverick had nothing to say to anyone. Jester and Viper, wrapped in towels, walked by the bench where they were dressing. "You know," Jester said casually, "that was the best flying I've seen since Nam." He grinned at Maverick, then turned back to Viper and kept on walking. "Right up to the part where they got killed," he finished with a laugh.

When they had gone into the showers, Goose said,

"Well, anyway, the good news is that Viper got Iceman after he got us."

It wasn't very consoling. Maverick tried to smile but just ended up shaking his head and walking out of the locker room. Goose sat on the bench with hardly enough energy to get himself going. It had been a rough day. But it was going to be a great night. Suddenly, his face lit up and there was enough energy to take on the world. He was looking ahead. Carole and Bradley, tonight!

In the four years that Goose and Carole had been married, they'd only had a few months together, broken down into days, mostly, except for the time he was stationed in Pensacola and they were almost like normal people—that had lasted nearly four months. But oh, they loved each other a lot. Goose couldn't think of a time when he hadn't known Carole and loved her. They had chased chickens together as barefoot kids and gone all through high school holding hands. Carole was his lifeline and his reality. Riding to the airport to meet her that evening, Goose found the taxi unbearably slow and had to keep himself from urging the driver to step on it. There was plenty of time; he was just that eager to see them. One-and-a-half-year-olds could change a lot in two weeks; what if Bradley didn't even recognize him?

A thin, earnest young woman with long, lank hair and a skirt that dragged the floor of the airport tried to get their attention in the airport concourse. She handed them leaflets and asked urgently, "Do you know what you can do for the defense of America?"

Goose smiled genially at her and answered over his

shoulder as they strode by. "Yes, ma'am. Pay Navy pilots more money!"

They pressed past her and all the bustle of people coming and going, and Goose grew serious. "I tried to tell her not to come, you know. I mean, I'm busy all the time. Ass draggin' like an old, tired dog. Studyin' at night. Told her *you* didn't even have a woman here."

Maverick smiled. "Who's got time?" He shrugged. Waiting for Carole's plane to arrive, Goose kept looking out the window and pacing. Maverick settled back and watched him, wondering what it would be like to want and need someone that much. The flight was announced finally, and they moved up to the gate to watch the passengers coming off. A couple arguing. An elderly woman carrying too much. A harassed-looking young mother with a toddler by the hand and one in her arms was met by the kids' proud grandparents. A businessman. And then Carole appeared; she was a pretty country woman, direct and earthy, blooming with health and warmth. She was carrying a red-cheeked baby, who was sound asleep on her shoulder. Carole's face lit up when she spotted Goose.

"Nick!" He held her and the baby tightly, and as they hugged each other, Bradley woke up. He stared dizzily right into Maverick's face. Bradley grinned. Maverick winked at him. Then Goose took his son into his arms, hoisted him onto his shoulders, and was rewarded with a chuckle and two little hands that clapped together in glee. They all laughed; then Carole hugged Maverick and they all headed for the baggage claim, with young Bradley piloting by the hair of his daddy's head.

"Maverick! Goose told me on the phone he thought you were in love with one of your instructors! What gives?" Carole pumped him cheerily as they strode down the long walkway. Maverick was caught by total surprise—he stared around Carole to Goose, who broke into a run, whooping in unison with his delighted son.

"He's exaggerating, as usual," Maverick assured her. "Although she is awfully beautiful, and smart, and . . . nope. No, it's hopeless, Carole. She just hasn't got it, the one requirement I need." He shook his head as she stepped onto the escalator ahead of him.

Carole looked back up at him quizzically, knowing he was teasing, knowing she'd have to take the bait, anyway. "Now, what requirement is that, honey?"

"She's not from Buck Holler," he said sadly. "I could only ever love a girl from Buck Holler. I've known that ever since I first met you."

"Am I going to get a chance to meet her?" Carole asked, wisely ignoring his silliness.

"She's worried about fraternizing with the boys at school," Maverick said. "But maybe with you along as old married chaperones, she could be talked into it."

"Well, you try," Carole said. "I want to meet this person who's got you calling her beautiful. And smart. She must be a one."

"Yes," Maverick agreed. "She's a one, all right."

To Maverick's surprise, Charlie agreed to be seen in public with him, and the four of them had a terrific seafood dinner at a little hideaway restaurant right on the water. Then they went down the beach to a bar where music rolled softly enough so that conversation was possible. Carole and Charlie hit it off instantly, probably a classic case of opposites attracting. The mountain girl and the sophisticated Ph.D. aerophysics expert chatted together with unending interest. Charlie obviously liked Goose a lot too; she even laughed at his jokes. By the time they got to the bar, Goose was acting up, his high spirits stratospheric tonight. He was behind the counter, serving up the beers and enchanting the fat lady bartender, whose giggles rang through the room in contagious ripples of good cheer.

Carole, Maverick, and Charlie sat at a table and watched his antics. Carole didn't bother to hide the adoration she felt for that big, tall hick. Love shone from her eyes every time she looked at him. But finally she sighed in mock despair and turned to Maverick. "Would you go fetch him? God, Maverick, doesn't he ever embarrass you?"

Maverick stood up. "Goose? Heck, no . . . well . . . he did bring in some camel dung from Lebanon and paint it on my shoes just before a briefing in Washington. And there were the fabu—" He stopped himself, but Carole had picked up on what he was about to say and said it for him.

". . . fabulous Bisquayne sisters." She laughed.

"He *told* you about them!" Maverick said, astonished.

Carole nodded. "Oh, yes, the lingerie saleswomen? He tells me about all of them. And about how my little angel Goose goes home early for church. But you always go home with the hot women?"

Maverick grimaced, not wanting to look at Charlie, and walked over toward the bar, where, from the sound of it, Goose seemed to be goosing the fat lady.

Carole laughed and turned to Charlie. "I'd like to be able to warn you off about Maverick," she said, half seriously. Then she turned completely serious. "But I love him to death. He is decent, and kind, and open as a spring window. If he wasn't a pilot I'd run away with him in a minute. But I cannot abide pilots."

They both laughed at this. Maverick persuaded Goose to give up his promising career as a bartender and return to the table. They were heading this way. "I've known Pete for a lot of years now, and I'll tell you one thing for sure," Carole went on quickly. "There are hearts breakin' wide open all over the world tonight."

Intrigued, still laughing, Charlie asked, "Why?"

"Because unless you're a fool—and you don't dress like one—that boy is off the market. He is totally, one hundred percent, prime-time in love with you."

Charlie liked that, and Carole was relieved to see it. Then Maverick and Goose were at the table with them. Carole looked up at her husband. "Goose, you big stud, take me to bed or lose me forever!" She leaned over to Charlie as she got up from the table and said loudly, "He likes me to give him confidence like that. God knows they need it, built funny like they are!"

When Charlie's big, beautiful laughter rang out, Carole reached down and hugged her happily. "I like you, lady," Charlie told her. "This is gonna be fun."

Goose put his arm tightly around his wife and started to lead her away. She turned back for a second to plant a quick kiss on Maverick's cheek. "Oh, boy, feel the heat!" she murmured, and then they were leaving. Carole pulled Goose by his belt and led him toward the door. The fat lady behind the bar was convulsed with pleasure as everyone shouted good-bye and *adios*.

Maverick sat down. He leaned back in his chair and smiled, closing his eyes. Charlie put her chin in her hand, elbow on the table, and looked at him long and hard. In a minute, he opened his eyes and looked at her. It seemed to her there was love in that look.

"I wish I were more like her," she said softly.

"She is special, isn't she?" he agreed. They kept on gazing into each other's eyes. Charlie nodded.

"So are you," Maverick said. "That's how I see you."

"Like Carole? Like that?" she asked.

Maverick nodded. "That's how I see you," he avowed solemnly.

"I appreciate that," she answered. Then she couldn't help giggling. Maverick just watched her, enjoying every moment. The giggling turned wild, and then she was laughing so hard she could hardly get the words out one at a time.

"Maverick, you big stud, take me to bed or lose me forever!"

He loved her so much that he almost melted right then and there. Somehow, though, he found the strength to do as she asked.

Chapter 15

SHE CLUNG TO him tightly as he gunned the bike across the desert to the coast highway, then cut across to the beach, racing the incoming tide along the hard, wet sand lit by moonlight, the salt spray in their faces and her exhilarated laughter in his ear, the wide sky overhead. He felt her arms around his waist, saw her scarf flying in the wind, sensed her heart opening like a wildflower. And then there was only the silent moonlight, beaming down like a blessing on them, out on the deck of her house. They made love with the sensuous surf breaking only yards away, all the world in harmony with their feelings for each other.

Finally they fell into the deep, brief, grudging sleep of lovers. At dawn, Maverick caught the fresh bite of the morning air deep in his lungs and found himself grinning idiotically as he sped back to the base.

Preflight instructions: ". . . Mig sweep over the water . . . you will proceed down the one-seven-zero-degree radial looking for Migs . . . you will engage all that you find, destroy them, and return to base. Maverick has the lead. Any questions? All right, let's go. Move like you've got a purpose."

"How do you read me, Goose?"

Goose punched open the intercom switch with his left foot. "Loud and clear. Have a good time last night?"

"Left console—radio off. TACAN off. AWD-nine liquid-cooling switch off."

"Check."

"Panel—ground test panel covered. NAV mode switch off. AWG-nine power off. IFF transponder—damn, this thing is hard to reach—okay, it's off."

"Check. Just want to make sure the lady is treating you well."

"Canopy is coming closed. All clear?"

"All clear."

The Plexiglas canopy came down and fastened securely around them. Maverick started the engines, and their ICS was temporarily shut out as the cockpits began to pressurize. Both men had long ago learned the trick of waiting to put their masks on until this phase was over—it helped to be able to yawn, to clear their ears while the pressure was building. Maverick found he wanted to rub his eyes, as well.

The plane captain stood alongside the front cockpit, signaling as various stages of the start-up procedure progressed. With both engines running, Maverick did his check of the emergency generator. All okay.

Goose reached to his left of the console to push a yellow and black lever forward. "Pilot" position now gave Maverick complete discretion on the ejection command.

Goose pushed the AWG-9 liquid-cooling switch to the rear and the AWG-9 power switch forward.

"TACAN on—check. Radio on—check. IFF—stand by."

After a moment, Maverick confirmed. "Proceed with OBC."

Goose rotated the category knob on the console-mounted keyboard to SPECIAL, and punched the ON BOARD CHECK button. The radar screen in front of him, twin to the one in the front cockpit, came alive with columns of data as the systems were individually run through the automatic check. When the report was completed, he set the altimeter, lined up the inertial navigation system, entered his waypoint data, performed the TACAN BIT, switched the NAV mode to INS, and gave the go-ahead to take off.

Maverick thumbed-up the plane captain and they began to roll. Within seconds, they were leveling out at 20,000 feet, just over a cover of thick white clouds. Three others came up to join them, and the four Tomcats skimmed sweetly in tight formation, plunging through the clouds and skimming over the Pacific in search of Migs.

"Bogey at nine o'clock," Iceman reported tersely. All four jets went into action, performing exactly by the book, covering each other, watching for the other Migs, spotting and engaging. They flew scissors patterns, slashing past each other, angling for position. The air was abuzz with voices, pilot-to-RIO, plane-to-plane—a barrage of information. Modern sounds of battle readiness, not so different from the sharpening of arrows or the clinking of stones in other times.

Iceman swung close to Maverick, wing-to-wing. They made eye contact, just a glance, and exchanged a curt nod, acknowledging the challenge. At 15,000 feet, traveling at 375 knots, the fight was on. Conscious mostly of each other, the two pilots were too good to let their real attention waver from the larger fight. Suddenly an F-5 shot out of the clouds directly in front of them.

The bogey was on the Iceman's starboard wave; smoothly, like an automatic reflex, Iceman rolled in on him. "On bogey," he announced. "I can get him in thirty degrees more."

Iceman's plane was rolled out on the other side of the bogey now, maneuvering to come in again, but Maverick could have him easily. "I'm in a good position to come in right now!" he told Iceman, and to Goose he added, "Shit! If that fucker would get out of there, I could get in!"

The F-5 ducked, a hard left turn that got him away from Iceman's oncoming roll. "He still hasn't got him," Maverick muttered. But there were rules; it was Iceman's bogey until he backed off, and all Maverick could do was sweat and swear and hang around to cover. Iceman was struggling against five and a half Gs to bring his nose to bear. The two planes went around into a Lufbery—that tight circle that air circus audiences love because it makes them gasp. Iceman had the advantage—he was closer to the bogey's tail than the F-5 was to his. But he couldn't close, couldn't line up the shot. Maverick hung in near enough so that he could see the Iceman groaning and straining against the fierce forces of gravity that were pushing him down.

"I can come in right here," he said urgently.

"Stay where you are!" Iceman spat back, laboring to get the words out. "I need . . . another twenty degrees, then I've . . . got him."

"Shit!" Maverick grunted. "I'm in a good position to come in right now!" he repeated pointedly.

"Just . . . five seconds," Iceman answered. But he still wasn't in a good position on the F-5.

Maverick blew his stack. "Fire it or clear out! That's enough of this bullshit. I can get him, Ice. I'm in right now. Come off high right!"

Pulling a lot of Gs, Maverick was having his own problems targeting his weapons; having Iceman in the middle was no help. Maverick kept turning in a hard circle, going round and round without gaining on the F-5. He couldn't bring his nose to bear as long as the Iceman was in the way. Maybe they were having the same problem; maybe it wouldn't be any easier without that jerkoff up here, but it sure as hell wasn't going to happen this way. "I'm in, Ice," he warned. "Come off high right!"

But the Iceman stayed. "No . . . just five seconds," he said.

Maverick dived down between the two planes, pulling 6.5 Gs, exposing his underside to Iceman, losing visual contact with him.

"Roger," Iceman conceded. "I'm out. Fuck!" He slammed the stick hard—an extraordinary loss of control for the cool and collected by-the-book Iceman, a moment of anger to which the plane responded before he could call it back. He was headed straight up toward Maverick.

"Look out!" Ice shouted, unable to divert his course.

Maverick saw the glinting flash of Iceman's plane suddenly filling his view. He slammed the stick forward, avoiding collision by no more than inches. It was terrifyingly close. He heard Goose protest, "Oh, no!" and then they were passing through the Iceman's turbulence. The blast distorted the airflow to Maverick's left engine . . . *boomboomboomboom*—the engine flamed out. With the full thrust on the right, the engine swung the tail around in a yaw. Maverick slammed the stick hard right to correct, but it was too late.

"Plane's coupling up!" Goose yelled. "Plane's coupling up!"

The plane coupled one yaw to the next—swinging the tail around—which became an ever-increasing flat spin, out of control.

"This is not good!" Goose drawled, trying to retain his calm demeanor against a rising panic—and almost succeeding. "We're low!"

Centrifugal force pinned Maverick to the instrument panel. Desperately, he forced his right arm back to try to reach the ejection lever, but his grasp fell short by at least six inches. "I'm pinned to the panel," he told Goose.

"Time to go," Goose said.

"I can't eject!"

The plane was spinning faster and faster, speed increasing as the spiral took them down. Maverick managed to pull the lever that dropped the landing gear, but nothing slowed the momentum of the spin.

"Three thousand feet," Goose reported. "I'll do it for you."

Back in the rear cockpit, he was closer to the center of the spin and consequently receiving less G-force. He switched over from pilot operation and reached behind him for the eject handle.

"Go ahead," Maverick said. "I can't reach. Two thousand feet!"

Ejection initiated. Shoulder harnesses retracted. Suddenly a blast of wind and noise, deafening, as the canopy hooks were cut and the bubble of Plexiglas was ballistically jettisoned. But instead of soaring off on its own, the canopy hovered just above their heads, spinning crazily, held by the vortex of the sinking jet.

"One thousand," Goose said. "Watch that canopy!"

"Let's go. Eject!"

Goose yanked the handle. Everything happened in a split second: the catapult fired, leg restraints were pulled taut, drogue gun and time-release mechanism were tripped. The second officer's seat was set to trigger first, the pilot's seat following four-tenths of a second later. The rocket under Goose's seat fired him up and out; almost instantly he impacted the spinning canopy with a sickening *crunch*. The canopy was knocked away. Maverick was slammed back into his seat as the ejection seat straps wound up, and then he was blasted out of the plane.

He didn't lose consciousness, but the shock made him feel drugged, out of it. The sudden silence—the plane must have hit the water and was now soundlessly sinking deeper and deeper into the bottomless Pacific . . . the sensation of floating through the air in slow, silent motion . . . where was Goose—no, don't think about that. Ejection sequence, finish ejection sequence, that was Rule Number One. That first, then . . . the horror. Later.

There should have been nothing but the silence now, as he tumbled over and over, head over boots. But a scream echoed in his head, over and over and over— Goose's scream as his head hit the canopy. It echoed and wouldn't stop. And the deafening thump of his own heart beating, and his own labored breathing; he was still alive. Goose was screaming over and over and over—

There had been no time for the time-release escapement mechanism to function, not enough altitude. Maverick groped for straps but found he was still attached to the seat. Wildly, he reached for the shackle and yanked it. The line stretch of the main chute freed him, and the seat fell away. His body snapped like a bullwhip as the chute ballooned open over his head. He drifted for only a moment and then hit the water, hard. He was dragged under, still tumbling, down and down in the cold, salty water that turned blacker as it pulled him deeper and deeper into the bottomless sea.

He hadn't expected the plunge so soon; he had no air in his lungs; he was going to suffocate or drown. He choked and gasped and sank heavily. Abruptly, with a force that churned the water, his body was yanked to one side. He felt himself helplessly being dragged through the water. His parachute had been caught by the wind above the surface, and it was dragging him along. His hands groped wildly but found nothing to hold onto. The need to breathe was agonizing. He twisted his body desperately, trying to slip out of the tangled straps, feeling that his lungs would burst. His hand grasped the lines, and he tried frantically, with strength he didn't think he had, to swim up the lines without pulling them down. Follow the lines, they would lead him up . . . endlessly far, no light at the surface, nothing but blackness and then, almost exploding, Maverick rose to the surface of the water.

He sucked the air into his lungs, surprised to find them still remembering what to do with it. Weak as a baby, he reached back for the release straps and somehow managed to break free from the parachute. It whipped away like a kite, free and out of sight in an instant, on its way to the sun.

The sea was choppy, four- to six-foot waves. The survival equipment was heavy and waterlogged, trying to drag him down again. He twisted, found the inflatable raft attached to his harness, and pulled its cord. The raft hissed open, six feet long and two feet wide, attached to him by a cord. He hoisted himself onto it and collapsed, completely exhausted.

The survival had been almost without thinking: an instinctive physical struggle. He slept, tossing on the waves, the sun beating down on him, a scream still echoing in his head.

When he came to, the sun was setting below the horizon and twilight was settling down over the vast ocean. He sat up and began a check of the situation. The dye tube was intact; he stained the water. There was the paddle, but not much point in starting to row toward California. He scanned the surface in all directions for a sign of anything: debris from his plane, a ship heading his way, any sign of life. He spotted an oil slick, pieces of honeycomb titanium, and then—a parachute, waterlogged and floating on the surface. He grabbed the paddle and maneuvered his raft toward it as fast as he could manage. It swelled away from him, then back, up on another wave—he rode the surf neatly and caught up with it. He reached over the side and frantically began to pull on the heavy submerged cords.

It was a great struggle. The weight was more than his own; time and again he almost lost momentum to the great downward pull as he hauled and hoisted and struggled against the terrible weight of it. It was almost dark when Maverick finally pulled Goose to the surface.

Maverick released the parachute. He pulled Goose

into the raft on top of him and held Goose in his arms. He stared into Goose's face; Goose was dead. He held him, rocked him with the rhythm of the little raft on the waves, weeping, keening his anguish and sorrow to the stars.

Faintly, and then more strongly, he heard something else alive out there—the beating of a helicopter's wings and the drone of its engines. Lights appeared in the distance; a searchlight was playing over the water several miles away. Maverick couldn't get at his harness pocket without letting go of Goose, but it was okay, He unzipped his RIO's survival pouch and pulled out a pencil flare. Holding it high, he popped it into the air. The chopper turned toward them. Within a few minutes, the flicking blades were directly over the raft. The chopper lowered its lights, scanning and finding the debris, zeroing in on Maverick and Goose in their raft.

The draft from the chopper churned the water. A frogman dropped from above into the water with a heavy splash; he surfaced and swam toward the raft, disappearing between each wave and then reappearing ever closer until he arrived alongside. The chopper lowered a rescue harness; it dropped into the water and the frogman grabbed onto it. Maverick held tightly to Goose and watched the operation as though it had nothing to do with him.

The frogman looked at Maverick, then at Goose. He started to examine Goose more closely. Maverick hugged his partner closely to himself; instinct again, no thinking, just an inability to let go. They were frozen together.

"Let him go, sir. Take it easy," the frogman said.

He tried to pry Goose free, but Maverick had him in a death-grip.

"Sir! Let him go! It's all right. Let him go!"

Maverick glared at the stranger bobbing in the water. Then the fog of shock and horror lifted for a moment. He let go of Goose. The frogman quickly strapped Maverick into the harness. As he was being hoisted up, he stared down at the lifeless body in the raft, growing smaller and smaller in the vast black expanse of water. Maverick, coming back to life despite himself, shivered from the bitter cold.

Chapter 16

MAVERICK COULD HEAR them talking but he didn't care what they said or what they did; it had nothing to do with him. He was listening to Goose's screaming, not to Viper and Jester outside the open door of his hospital room. They were speaking low but he could hear them anyway. It didn't matter.

"The Board of Inquiry people are already on top of it. We asked them to expedite this one because of graduation." That was Jester. Maverick heard his footsteps walking away. He thought maybe he should call Jester back and tell him not to sound so concerned, that it really didn't matter. But he couldn't say anything or care.

Viper came into his room and stood over his bed. Maverick met the CO's probing look with blank, expressionless eyes.

"How do you feel?" Viper asked him calmly, quietly.

"All right," Maverick answered.

"Goose is dead."

"I know." He felt nothing. Dead people felt nothing.

Viper's face was strained, aging. "If you fly jets long enough," he said with vast weariness, "something like this happens. No one escapes it."

Maverick heard the words. Was the CO trying to say it didn't matter? "He . . . he was my . . . my responsibility . . . my RIO," he protested.

Viper nodded sadly. "My first squadron in Vietnam, we lost eight out of eighteen planes. Ten guys. The first one, you die, too . . . but there'll be others. You can count on it."

Maverick didn't react at all. He didn't want to hear about others. He could still hear Goose's screaming as his head hit the canopy.

"You've got to put him in the box, son," Viper said, not unkindly.

Maverick looked at him but had nothing to say.

Charlie came to see him, but they had no privacy and no time to say anything because the medics were so busy working him over. Maverick couldn't think of anything to say to her, anyway. He didn't want to feel happy to see anyone, but he didn't mind her promise to come and get him when they let him out. The doctors tested him for everything they could think of and said he was okay. The psychiatrist thought he ought to come in from time to time, if he felt the need to talk, and Maverick said he would, sure.

It was night again when they said he could leave, and Charlie was there with her car. He just got in without saying anything, and she drove straight to the barracks. She pulled into the parking lot, turned off the ignition, but left the radio on, very softly. It was playing John Lennon: "Stand By Me."

They sat for a while, making no effort to talk or move. He leaned his head against the seat and closed his eyes.

"They say you're all right," she said.

He opened his eyes. "Good."

"It's going to take time," she said gently. She waited for him to say something, but he had nothing to say. "I've been with Carole and the baby. She's wonderfully tough—in the best sense of the word, I mean. She's always known it could happen, she said. A flier's wife . . . knows it can happen anytime. She's going to be all right."

Maverick nodded. He couldn't say anything.

"I know it doesn't seem possible now, but time will help. You need to put as much life as you can between it and you. Time's the only miracle," she told him quietly.

"If it's a miracle," he said, "I want it back."

"What?"

"Yesterday," Maverick answered. His voice was flat, but there were tears close to it. "I want him in there. Here."

Charlie reached out her hand to touch his. "Look," she said softly, "what you do is really dangerous. It could have been you."

"It wasn't me. It was my hand. My brain. My fault."

"You believe that?"

She was so easy to be with, easy to talk to, he could almost find words to express what he meant. "When I breathe in," he said, "it was my fault. When I breathe out . . . I don't know."

She held his hand. She seemed to understand what he couldn't say. Maybe.

"I have to spend some time alone," Maverick told

her. "I need to think this out." He could only hope her understanding would stretch this far. "Okay?" he asked flatly.

Charlie nodded. She let go of his hand, but then she touched his arm lightly, as if she wanted to let go but couldn't. "Maybe you can stop thinking," she said.

Maverick opened the car door. "Not quite yet," he said.

Charlie nodded again. " 'Night, Maverick," she whispered.

He watched her drive away and then he turned to go into the barracks. Two nights ago she had been the most important person in the world, in the universe. Maybe that had been the mistake . . . the guy in the other cockpit of your plane is the most important . . . he still heard Goose's scream when his head hit that whirling canopy, still felt the weight of Goose's dead body in his arms.

Nobody in the halls. He didn't know how they would treat him, what they would think, and it didn't matter. His footsteps sounded loud and lonely as he approached Goose's room. He stopped at the door, then turned the knob and went inside. He stood for a moment in the dark, then forced himself to cross the narrow room to the desk, reach over, and switch on the lamp.

There was an empty cardboard box on the closet floor. Goose had been moving his stuff, a few things at a time, to the apartment since Carole's arrival, filling it up—mostly with books—and bringing it back empty for another load. He hadn't had time to move everything.

Slowly, Maverick began to gather Goose's personal possessions. Each thing became the subject of intense scrutiny and thoughtful handling, almost as though he might find some message or meaning in a shirt, a pair of shoes, books, a traveling alarm clock, a Walkman, or toilet articles from the bathroom. He let go of each thing reluctantly, fumbling it into the box. He couldn't see very well. His eyes were full of tears.

Carole opened the door for him and sort of smiled. Maverick held the box under his arm. She saw it and reached for it. The television was on, but neither of them knew it. Awkwardly, he put the box in her hands.

"God, he loved flying with you, Maverick," she said.

Maverick gasped and hugged her, box and all, and he held on tightly for a long moment. Then she pulled back and eyed him directly. "But he'd a flown anyway. Without you. He'd hate it, but . . . he'd do it."

It was like a sock in the chops. She was telling him to go ahead and keep on flying *without Goose!* But he couldn't do that. He was sure he couldn't do that. He couldn't even talk about that. He just had to turn and walk away from her. He heard baby boy Brad calling "Mama" from the bedroom as he went out the door.

". . . disregard of . . . basic air-safety principles . . ."

". . . too aggressive . . ."

". . . incident twenty-nine July . . ."

". . . within performance parameters . . ."

". . . disciplinary action . . . tactical doctrine . . ."

". . . even reckless at times . . ."

". . . only conjecture . . ."

". . . unsupported . . . benefit of the doubt . . ."

The voices were far away, unreal. Maverick sat like a wooden soldier, all dressed up in his whites, with gold and navy stripes on his shoulder boards, gold buttons and a braid on the cap he held in his dry, still hands. His eyes were downcast, dark lashes hiding the fact that he stared at nothing. The rumbling voices came and went in his ears, never touching his mind. It was getting to be a permanent condition, and so was not caring.

"Lieutenant Mitchell!"

Loud and clear. He responded to his name. His eyes focused slowly. The room swam into view; all the officers were staring at him, and they were real. Most of them were sitting behind two long tables at the other end of the room. There was a Navy commander in the center. Viper was there, too, not behind the table but seated in front and to one side.

The commander looked at Maverick and spoke solemnly, officially, for the record: "The Board of Inquiry finds that Lieutenant Pete Mitchell was not at fault in the accident of twenty-nine July."

Maverick heard him. He didn't respond. He was aware of Viper studying his face, but he didn't know what Viper was looking for. Maverick kept looking at the commander and trying to make sense out of what he was saying.

"Lieutenant Mitchell's record will be cleared of this incident."

Okay.

"Lieutenant Mitchell is restored to flight status without further delay. These proceedings are closed," the commander said. The officers stirred and the commander stood up. Maverick just sat there, still not responding.

Viper had seen this before. He leaned over to Jester, who was sitting behind him. "Get him up flying soon or forget it," the CO whispered.

Jester nodded. He had seen it, too. "Yes, sir!" he

agreed. He got up and walked over to the chair where Maverick sat. "Let's go, Maverick," he snapped.

Maverick let himself be guided out of the inquiry room and back to the barracks. He stepped out of the car and seemed to wait for others. "Flight suits and see you on the line in twenty minutes!" Jester snapped. "Lots of catching up to do, Maverick!"

Maverick nodded and went into the barracks. He went to his room and dressed, automatically, not thinking, trying not to feel. Twenty minutes later he was on the line, sitting in a cockpit and staring at the controls.

Sundown was flying RIO with him today. He was suited up and ready, just waiting for Maverick to get there before climbing aboard. He shook Maverick's hand and pulled his cap over the wisps of singed red hair just growing back after his misfortune with the Flaming Hooker. The ground crew was all over the plane, prepping. Coogan strapped Maverick in, saying kind words, encouraging words that Maverick couldn't really hear over the jet roar and radio babble. The cockpit looked like alien territory, suddenly foreign to him. He put his right hand forward and touched the stick. It looked like a primitive ebony carving, thick and curved and obscene. Maverick turned to look over his shoulder at the twin tails. He seemed surprised to discover that moving the stick had an effect on the control surfaces in the tails. Sundown started the drill:

"How do you read me, Maverick?"

"Loud and clear," he answered automatically. And then they continued down the checklist, with Sundown's strange voice saying Goose's lines: "Brakes—brakes okay. Fuel—sixteen thousand pounds. Canopy—handle closed, hooks engaged. Seat—all armed forward . . ." On and on, by rote, until they were airborne and Maverick found himself flying again.

Gear went up and in seconds they were level at 1,000 feet, with flaps coming up. Maverick banked left and waited for his wingman; then he turned and flew steady on the predetermined course. Cruising at 15,000 feet, 300 knots, they maneuvered and patrolled until suddenly Sundown called out: "Bogey at ten o'clock low. You've got the angle on him—piece of cake!"

Maverick checked out ten o'clock low—but the F-14 stayed on its course. In that one instant of not responding, Maverick became a man with no secret: he was afraid.

"Engage, Maverick—anytime!" Sundown urged.

Abruptly, the bogey turned toward them. Maverick hesitated again. Then he jerked the stick hard right, running the Tomcat away from the bogey with a burst of speed that jolted them with another full G.

"What? Where're you going—what the hell—hey, where in hell are you going?" Sundown shouted excitedly.

"Didn't . . . ahhh . . . didn't look good," Maverick answered lamely.

"What do you mean? It doesn't *get* to look much better than that!" Sundown was outraged.

"No," Maverick answered firmly. "No good."

No more chances today. They headed home in silence, except for the landing checks. Maverick could feel Sundown's disappointment zeroed on the back of his head from behind, but that was Sundown's problem. It was only one day's score for Sundown; he'd go back to his own pilot tomorrow and somebody else would get the immense pleasure of riding with the killer Maverick.

Once on the ground and unstrapped, Maverick walked away from the plane as quickly as he could. He felt sick. But Sundown, still getting out of his rig, called to him from the rear cockpit.

"We had a good shot, Maverick," he said accusingly.

Maverick spun around on his heels and strode back to the plane. Frustrated, angry, embarrassed, and wild, he shouted up, "You call 'em from the backseat, I shoot 'em from the front, *when I'm ready!*"

Jester was watching from a few yards away. Shaking his head, the leader walked over to an F-5, where Viper was standing. "He can't get back on the horse, Skipper. He just won't engage."

"It's his first shot. Give him a few days," the CO answered.

"I've seen this before," Jester said.

"So have I."

"Some guys never get it back."

Viper nodded thoughtfully. He watched Maverick walking off the field. Well named, this unruly colt might turn any which way, might buck and rear . . . or might never get his spirit back, if it had been truly broken. It was dangerous to count on a man like that. His life, other lives, another thirty-million-dollar airplane—the stakes were immense. Could the maverick get himself back? No one else could do it for him.

Viper thought very carefully. He had known Maverick's father. But it wasn't sentiment that made him decide.

"Keep sending him up," he ordered.

Chapter 17

ICEMAN WAS COMBING his immaculate hair. The small mirror over the locker-room sink hardly did justice to the amount of attention he paid it; it reflected back a crooked image of a very straight fellow. Iceman seemed to be operating on the principle that if he combed neatly enough, the mirror would salute. Hardly anything would distract him from this momentary obsession, but when Maverick came in, he looked over at him. So did everyone else in various stages of undress.

Maverick opened his locker, pulled out his duffel bag, and started to throw things into it, ignoring everyone, oblivious even to Iceman's stare. But Iceman didn't let it rest. He walked over and stood behind Maverick, watching him. Finally he spoke, getting right to the point. "Everybody liked Goose." Maverick didn't turn around. Iceman began to move away, but stopped, and, over his shoulder, said, "I'm sorry." Then Iceman walked away and, for a moment, Maverick was totally alone.

"Hey, Maverick?" Wolfman came lumbering over and stood, half in and half out of his G-suit, scratching his head and sounding as concerned as he was curious. "What are you doing?"

"Saving them some paperwork," Maverick said. He pulled a pair of running shoes out of his locker and stuffed them down into the bag. He ran his hand around the inside of the locker to see if he'd overlooked anything.

"Since when did you care about paperwork?" Wolfman asked.

Maverick zipped up the canvas bag, picked it up, and walked toward the door. After a minute's hesitation, Wolfman, his unzipped leggings flapping, came after him. Iceman was concentrating on his mirror again; the other men in the locker room seemed very busy doing their own things, all of a sudden. Wolfman had to quicken his step to catch up, not an easy thing when you've got a G-suit hanging around your waist like a half-zipped corset. He hobbled after Maverick and caught up with him just outside the door.

"If I could fly like you, I'd have everything I want. If I could fly at all. I can't fly like that. Nobody can. Whatever it is, you've got it," he pleaded urgently.

"Had it," Maverick corrected him, tight-lipped.

Wolfman reached for the handle of the duffel bag, wresting it away from Maverick in an attempt to make him stop walking. "You're scared," he said. "So what? No one ever gets a good look at any fighter pilot when he's flying. They're either scared or . . . or they're bad pilots! I'm goddamned *terrified!*"

Maverick eyed him and nodded, by way of saying *thanks for trying*. He took back the canvas bag from Wolfman and turned to go on down the hall. Jester was coming out of the locker room; Maverick brushed past him and kept going. Wolfman and Jester watched him go. Then, sighing and shaking his kind, teddy-bear head, Wolfman went back inside the locker room. He stopped at the pay phone that was just inside the door.

He checked with the listings posted alongside the phone and dialed an extension. "Hello, Miss . . . uh . . . Charlie? This is Wolfman. I know it's not supposed to be any special concern of yours, but Maverick just took all his gear out of his locker and I think he's quitting. I mean, what he said was he was saving them paperwork. I thought you might—no, I think he's probably already on his way to the airport. I'd guess he wouldn't have gone into the locker room at this particular time if he could have put it off till the place was empty . . . my hunch is he maybe has a plane to catch, a civilian plane, you know? Yeah, you're welcome. I hope you catch him. You're a peach, Charlie. Huh? Oh, yes, ma'am. I know I'm not supposed to know. Nobody is. I wouldn't have called, except I think it's kind of an emergency and I thought you'd want—yes, ma'am. 'Bye." He hung up, vastly relieved.

The San Diego airport is huge and crowded—odds on finding someone—unless you know where to look— are not great. Charlie tried three newsstands and a coffee shop before her deductive powers took over and she headed for the bar. He was sitting alone at a table, his suitcase beside him; he was staring into a drink.

She hadn't seen him since the night he'd come out of the hospital; she was shocked at the change in him after only a couple of days. His ruddy tan had turned almost pale; his keen, bright eyes were downcast and grieving; the mouth she couldn't resist had gone slack. She took a very deep breath, putting down her fear that he might resent and hate her for interfering. Then she walked over to him and sat down across the little table from him.

"Is this the elephants' graveyard?" she asked.

He looked up. She could tell he wanted to be angry, but he couldn't—not with her. He gave her a small, grudging, sweet, crooked smile that flipped her heart over.

"I never thought you'd give up this easily," she said. "On women, maybe. But F-Fourteens?"

The waitress came over to them, bored and impatient. She crossed her arms and waited.

"I'll have what he's having," Charlie said, indicating Maverick's drink with her thumb. "Hemlock, is it?" she added sweetly. The waitress didn't smile or look curious. She just nodded and turned toward the bar.

It just wasn't funny, nothing about it was. Charlie leaned toward him. "You weren't going to say good-bye?" she asked quietly.

Maverick looked up from the little paper napkin he was twisting with his fingers. Their eyes caught, but it was a meeting of polite acquaintances. "Were you going to tell me about your new job in Washington?" he countered.

Charlie sighed. "Yes, I was. And I sure wasn't going to leave without . . . seeing you."

"I didn't want to see you . . . I mean, I did . . . but . . . I didn't . . ." Maverick's voice wavered and he shook his head as if to clear it. His dark eyes were miserable and Charlie wanted desperately to take him in her arms and hold him until the pain went away.

"Say," she said softly, "who's in charge inside there?"

They didn't even notice the waitress, who set two vodka tonics down in front of them.

Maverick's pained vulnerability gave way to brittleness and the anger came rushing in to cover his feelings. "Big talk for someone who never has crashed in her computer."

Charlie was stung. Her own fighting instincts took over before she realized it. "Hey! I never said I was a fighter pilot! I can find contentment in a good book. I don't have to roar by someone at Mach Two with my hair on fire. Sometimes . . ." She looked at him. "Sometimes," she went on in a softer tone, "I can just get happy being with the right man."

"I hope you find him," Maverick said.

"I thought I had," she answered softly.

Maverick shook his head. "You didn't find the right man, you found a juicy job. That's what you wanted and that's what you got yourself. Right?"

"Right," she agreed. "I asked about your Mig and you read me like a book. You know, I was afraid to ask about anything else—your father, your dog, your favorite socks. For fear I'd go and do what I went and did . . . get involved with some kid who doesn't know he's not living in Camelot."

Maverick was listening. He had stopped playing with the twisted paper napkin, and his hands were still. They were good hands, firm and strong, and they could be gentle, too. She could hardly bear to look at his mouth because it was saying hurtful things. "Well, you got the Mig. You got the job."

"And you woke up," she retorted. "You're not a knight in a kid's storybook. There are damned few happy endings anymore. Those are dangerous arrows you carry around. Terrible things happen. When people fall from great heights, they die. You can't bring them back."

Maverick closed his eyes suddenly. Charlie didn't know if he did it to block her out, the things she was saying, or to listen up and think about it. She found herself holding her breath, waiting for him to say something.

"That's not it," he said finally.

More gently, she asked, "What is it then?"

Maverick waited a long time before he answered. It was very difficult for him. But he wanted to tell her—he just didn't know how. "I'm . . . empty," he said. "I just don't think I can bring *me* back."

Charlie nodded. "I can understand that. I wish I could help you with it . . . oh, how I wish I could! But—I'm leaving here, and, I guess . . . so are you." She reached out to touch his arm. "But, Maverick . . . Pete . . . you do have a safety net. It's called the rest of the human race—your team, your wingmen. That's what I think a lot of people have been trying to bang into your head for a long time."

Maverick was silent for so long that Charlie thought maybe it was all he was willing to listen to. She felt like crying, but she put the feeling far away and resigned herself to the reality she had been urging on him. People got hurt, but they had to go on living. She stood up.

"I'm sorr—" Maverick started to say, but she interrupted him quickly.

"No apologies." She started to leave. "Well, that's it, I guess," she said. "I'm leaving. Just remember two things. If you're not Top Gun, if you're not fighting jets, you're not going to be able to *act* like a fighter pilot. You're going to have to act like the rest of us.

You're going to have to master humility. For you guys, that's the toughest maneuver of all."

She smiled ruefully down at him and turned to move away.

"What's the other thing?" Maverick asked.

She looked back at him, waited until she could take a deep breath and feel some modicum of control, and then she said, looking straight into his eyes, "Just in case sometime, somewhere, the question crosses your mind . . . the answer is I loved you. And you were worth it." Something sparkly gleamed in her eye for a moment. She went on, "So long, sailor. See you on the beach sometime."

As she walked through the crowded cocktail lounge, every male in the place watched her appreciatively, and some looked back at Maverick with obvious envy, but he couldn't see anything except the little shreds of paper he had torn apart on the table.

He sat for a long time. The loudspeaker may have called several flights that he might have taken, but he was thinking, and it was nearly impossible to hear what they were trying to say, anyway. He looked up once, in the direction that Charlie had gone. The waitress came around several times, but he hadn't touched the drink in front of him and didn't seem to hear her when she asked if he wanted another. People in airport bars did that sometimes; they were always killing time. Finally, the dark-haired young flier got up, put a bill down on the table, picked up his duffel bag, and walked out into the bustling, crowded concourse.

Chapter 18

HE DIDN'T EVEN know whether they'd take him back on the *Kitty Hawk*. The carrier was out in the Pacific somewhere; they might fly him out there and they might not. You couldn't just hop a flight on a whim when you were in the Navy—where had he been planning to go? Wherever he went now, for the rest of his career—if he had one—he'd be the hotshot who fucked up—badly. Really badly.

Maverick told the cab driver to take him to the Del Coronado beach—he'd have a drink, maybe check in at the famous old hotel and watch the surfers from the veranda, walk on the beach, think, and make a decision.

"You in the Navy?" the cabbie wanted to know.

Maverick just grunted, hoping the driver would get the message that he didn't feel real talky just now.

"I can always tell a Navy man. My son's in the Persian Gulf, on a destroyer. I was on a destroyer myself, three years in Korea. You're a flier, I'll bet."

"Yeah."

"I can always tell. You got the hardest job in the world, mister. My hat's off to you." He didn't have a hat, but with a jaunty hand he sent a sharp salute to the back seat. Maverick wished the guy would shut up and let him think. But the driver went on and on. "My son wanted to fly Navy, oh, boy, he always wanted to be a fighter pilot, you know? Always. But . . . well, like father, like son, you know what I mean? Funny how he ended up exactly where his old man did. Isn't it?"

Maverick had been trying to tune the guy out, but suddenly he looked at the back of the balding head. He heard the man's pride and his disappointment, too, and he looked at the rearview mirror to see the man's eyes.

"Maybe . . . he wanted to be like you. Do what you did. That's not so bad, is it?" he volunteered hesitantly. The driver's eyes in the mirror crinkled with pleasure.

"You understand a lot for a young kid," the driver said. "I always said fliers are the smartest. You got to be, I guess. But you're . . . wise, too, you know what I mean?"

"Not really." Maverick laughed, and the driver laughed, too. "Listen," Maverick said, leaning forward, "I want to make a phone call. I'm not sure I need to go to Coronado after all . . . can we stop at a phone someplace?"

"Sure thing. There's a drugstore right off this exit."

Maverick had to call Information first, and when he reached Viper's house, he was told in no uncertain terms that Viper didn't live there anymore.

"He's probably at the beach. Or the zoo, or the ball game," the woman who answered told him. She sounded angry.

"Oh," Maverick said, his voice falling. "You wouldn't know for sure which? I have to talk to him, ma'am. It's important."

"It always is, isn't it? Everything in the Navy is always more important than—oh, well, I'm sorry. Listen, every other Sunday he takes his son for the day, and usually they go to the beach. That's all I can tell you. Sometimes they go to the zoo, or the ball game."

"Yes, well, thank you."

The woman hung up in his ear. Maverick stood in the phone booth for a minute trying to decide what to do. Then, almost desperately, he phoned Information again. Sure enough, there was a separate listing for Viper, at the beach. There was no answer, but Maverick and his friend the cab driver headed out that way.

The CO was being led toward the water by a three-year-old kid who was clearly in command of the situation. The little boy had yellow hair bleached almost white by the sun, and deep nut-brown skin and red trunks that almost kept slipping off. He was tugging on Viper's hand and trying to pull him into the surf.

Maverick stood on the sand in front of Viper's house and watched them. The kid came about up to his father's knee, but he was winning the battle. Until Viper stopped in his tracks, said something, and pointed back to where Maverick was waiting for them. The little towhead grumbled but changed direction and came along.

He was chattering, apparently asking questions, all the way. As they came within earshot, Maverick heard him say, "Dad, of all the animals in the ocean, which one's the baddest?"

"I don't know, Tim," Viper answered. "You'll have to ask *them*."

As they reached Maverick, Tim broke away from his dad and started flying around the beach, arms outstretched, a three-year-old's approximation of jet engine noises sounding loud and healthy across the sand.

Viper grinned at him, then shrugged. "Runs in the family," he said to Maverick.

"I'm sorry to bother you, Skipper," Maverick apologized.

"No bother."

"I called your house . . . your wife said you took your kid to the beach every second Sunday. Or maybe the zoo, or the ball game. I wasn't sure I could find you."

Viper nodded, watching Tim still running around with his arms out like wings. "Beach or zoo, or the ball game," he said. "His option."

Maverick nodded. They both stood watching the little boy for a minute. Then Maverick asked, "Do I have options, too, sir?"

Viper turned to walk down the beach toward his son, and Maverick fell into step with him. "Your options? I thought you'd chosen."

Maverick looked down at the broken shells and kicked at a piece of driftwood.

"Well," Viper went on, "not many, I guess. We can send you back to your squadron with nothing noted on your record except C.N.C.—course not completed, no explanation required. Theoretically, it doesn't hurt your career, but people always wonder about things like that."

Maverick nodded. "Or?" he prompted.

"Or . . . you can quit. Which I thought you'd done. That's why I told Jester to prepare your papers."

Maverick's heart sank. Was that what he really wanted? Was it too late to change his mind—already? Tim had led them to an ice-cream stand; as wingmen to the child's imaginary plane, he and Viper came up on either side. After some serious consultation and a reading of the entire list of flavors, Viper ordered three chocolate cones.

"You've already made up your mind," Maverick said. He felt sick.

"No," Viper said thoughtfully. "That spin was hell." He sounded as if he were putting himself in Maverick's place—he sounded human, almost forgiving. "What happened to you—to your RIO—would shake anybody up. It's no disgrace, kid. The hard thing to do might be the right thing. Nobody can tell you that. But if you don't think you can cut it anymore, you *should* walk out."

Maverick felt his skin prickle and his blood start to race. "You think I should quit?"

Viper spoke calmly. He seemed as interested in watching the vendor scoop out the ice cream as Tim was. "I didn't say that," he told Maverick. "But I have a responsibility to the other guys up there, not just you. They need to know you're all right . . . that they can depend on you. You know that."

The vendor handed them the ice cream. "I'll get it," Maverick said. He reached into his pocket for change, pulled out a handful, and dumped it on the top of the wagon to count out the right amount. Viper's eye caught something, and he reached over, picking out the Navy Cross from under the dimes and quarters.

"Lucky charm," Maverick said shortly, reaching for it.

Viper shook his head. "Not in his case," he said. "He earned it."

Maverick had somehow figured that Viper might be one of the officers he encountered now and then who had known his dad. "You served with him?" he asked.

Viper nodded. "Flew with him, I'm proud to say."

Maverick felt the anticipation and anxiety he always experienced when the subject of his dad came up. Private memories, pride and the underlying fear that someone, someday, was going to destroy those memories and that pride by telling him something he didn't want to hear. He didn't say anything now; he just nodded.

They walked along the beach, Tim alongside his father now, holding hands and contentedly getting as much ice cream as he could manage into his mouth, the rest all over his entire body.

"VF Fifty-one, the Oriskany," Viper reminisced. "You remind me of him. You're just like he was, only better . . . and worse."

"I'm nothing like him," Maverick said sharply.

Viper chuckled. "That's the contrary sort of thing he'd say. He'd be wrong, too. You are like him."

"He was a team player," Maverick said shortly.

"He was a heroic, natural, flying son of a bitch. Yeah, he was a team player. Until he needed the juice right at the end. Then he flew like a demon. Saved a lot of guys' necks. Forgot about his own." Viper's voice was filled with emotion and he wasn't trying to hide it.

"I never heard that," Maverick said. It made his head spin.

"Not something they tell dependents."

"So he did it right?" Maverick asked. It was important for him to know. He found himself watching little Tim's sturdy legs as he ran along the sand to keep up with them. His dad was a flier, too. Maybe that kid had about as much chance to grow up knowing his dad as Maverick had had. He hoped the kid would be luckier than he had been. Than Goose's baby boy Bradley . . .

"He did it *very* right," Viper told him. "Just the wrong place for the State Department to acknowledge. We were over the wrong line on some map."

"You were there," Maverick said, a sense of wonder coming over him, a sense of . . . *closeness*.

"I was there," Viper assured him. "I'm here now because of him."

Maverick's ice cream had melted and run down, without his having taken a taste of it. He tossed it in a plastic garbage can near a lifeguard's station. Viper let his son lead them down to the water's edge, where they laughed and wrestled with the waves to get the kid clean. Maverick stood watching them, feeling emotions rush in where he had spent a lifetime pushing them back.

The three of them started to walk back along the water's edge, the boy running to challenge each wave and then squealing and giggling, just beating it back to dry land. "Kid," Viper said after a long, companionable silence, "the plain fact is that you feel responsible for Goose. And you've lost your confidence."

Maverick watched a tiny sand crab scurry for its hole. He didn't say anything, but waited for Viper to go on.

"Technically, the board of inquiry absolved you. I'm not going to stand here and blow sunshine up your ass. You and I know what really happened. You pushed it . . . and you'll carry that for the rest of your life. Now, the question is—what will you do with it? Maybe there is *some* value in it. It's the first thing I've ever seen that's really made you stop and question yourself."

Maverick was listening, thinking, trying to understand. "Does that mean you think I shouldn't fly?" he asked. There was no anger in it this time.

Viper shook his head. "A good pilot always questions himself. Stays alert to drifting. Makes little corrections."

He seemed to be finished. He called to Tim not to get too far ahead of them, and they stopped to pet a huge, wet, shaggy dog with a stick in her mouth. They were almost at Viper's house.

"Would you take me back?" he asked the CO. "Would they?"

Viper stopped walking and looked at Maverick long and hard. Tim ran to him and took his hand. "I don't know about me," Viper said frankly. "I start with what I know. You were gone. Now you're back. As for them, they've got a lot invested in you. They'd hate to lose it. The Navy needs a very few very, very good men."

Maverick reached out to shake his hand. Viper's grip was firm and somehow comforting, reassuring. Fatherly, almost. He said good-bye to Tim and headed out to the road to catch a ride back to the base.

Chapter 19

GRADUATION WAS A solemn and moving occasion—speeches and ceremonious reminders of what it was all about, a White House representative, two senators, and enough Navy brass to outglitz the sun, everybody in spanking whites and a special flyover to salute the new Top Guns. It was impressive, serious, and put lumps in more than a few throats. But when it was over and the hats were off, the celebration was as if somebody had lit the fuse on a Phoenix and it had just hit its target and blown sky-high.

Clusters of officers and their families chattered and laughed and hugged. They drifted off the lawn into the assembly room, where ceiling lights and celestial navigation charts and plaques and portraits of smiling Presidents and unsmiling admirals were incongruously decorated with streamers and balloons for the occasion. Jokes and insults were traded happily; all was good feeling, today. Every now and then, someone spoke of Goose, and a shadow passed along many faces, but for the most part, the mood was celebration, joy, pride, and camaraderie. The Iceman was the center of much attention, being ribbed and congratulated in about equal shares.

"Hey, Ice, I got you an offer to sell hair tonic on TV now that you're Top Gun."

"Yeah, they're going to show how he goes into Zone-five afterburn without ruffling a single hair on his head."

"Where's Maverick?" someone asked.

"Don't know where he is."

"What's he planning to do?"

Several guys shook their heads. It might have been any one of them. Maverick had changed a lot since Goose had bought it. The cocky, wise-guy battler was subdued, straight-arrow. He studied hard and he flew competently and he answered when somebody spoke to him, but there were bets taken on whether he'd last. The other fliers sympathized. They respected his feelings, and anybody who was assigned to fly RIO with him went willingly enough, but there were no volunteers.

Now that the pressure was off, the competition was over and they were all Navy, together. They ribbed each other, but they cared about each other and needed each other and they all knew it.

"It's got to be hard on the guy," someone said, and the others agreed. A flash camera went off, and heads turned toward the bar, where Iceman was standing in the center of a pretty good-sized group, proudly holding the Top Gun plaque and posing for a photo.

When Maverick came in, late and uncertain, he stood in the doorway for a moment, clearly not sure he wanted to be there. Hollywood spotted him, excused himself from the group he was with, and headed over.

"Greetings, graduate," he exclaimed heartily. Sundown was right behind him, freckled and grinning and offering beer. Maverick allowed himself to be led inside the room. He was trying to force himself to lighten up; he hoped he was smiling. He tried not to look in the direction of the center of attention—Iceman and his plaque.

"We did it—hey, Maverick?" Sundown said warmly, coming over to clasp an arm around his neck.

Wolfman spotted him and came over. The big bear raised his glass in a salute. "Glad you stuck it out, man," he said, meaning it.

One by one, others came up to Maverick and shook his hand. Everybody was shaking everybody's hand tonight, the survivors congratulating each other—and Maverick was a part of it. He saw Viper, who smiled and nodded a "thumbs-up" to him from across the room. He had hoped Charlie would be there, but she wasn't.

Maverick moved through the crowded room, smiling, talking, shaking hands, and looking for her . . . he thought he saw her, once, but it was another woman with blond hair that turned out not to be anything nearly as shiny and pretty as Charlie's hair. Someone thrust a beer in his hand and he raised it in a toast and took a swallow—and then he was aware of Jester, who wasn't smiling at all, and Viper, who was reading a message Jester had just handed him, and Viper wasn't smiling anymore, either. Suddenly there was a pall over the crowd, and the party seemed to quiet down as everyone in the room became aware that something was happening.

By the time Viper looked up and spoke to them, the whole room was hushed and waiting. "Gentlemen, you know how I hate to break up this party before it has had a chance to get really out of hand . . ." he said. Then, very seriously, he went on. "But there's a major flap on. You're moving out."

A rumble went through the group.

"Who is here?" Jester barked out. "Hollywood and Wolfman?"

"Yo!"

Jester quickly went down the list of teams, in pairs. All except Maverick, who didn't have a permanent RIO anymore. His name was called without a partner. "Maverick?"

"Yo!"

"All here, Skipper," Jester reported. He began handing out written orders as Viper explained as much as he could tell them.

"Someone's fired on one of our ships," the CO said. "You're on your way. You'll be on the *Kitty Hawk*, ready for orders, tonight. Don't bother going to the barracks—your bags are being packed and should be ready right now. I'm proud of you, men."

The teams had moved together in pairs during the roster. Viper looked over at Maverick, who was standing alone. He called out to him, "Maverick."

"Yes, sir."

"You'll get a RIO from your old squadron. And if you don't . . ."

Everyone in the room was listening hard.

". . . Give me a shout," the CO finished lightly. "I'll fly with you."

He meant it. Maverick nodded gratefully, filled with some indefinable emotion. Then he moved on out with the others.

* * *

They landed on the *Kitty Hawk* somewhere in the Pacific. When Maverick touched the wire and came to a stop, he was immediately told to report to Stinger for special instructions.

"You need a RIO," was all his old squadron leader said. "Preference?"

"Yes, sir. Merlin, if he'll fly with me." Merlin had been Cougar's RIO; he would have gone to Top Gun if everything hadn't gone so wrong in the beginning. Cougar and Merlin—that was the first-pick team. Only it hadn't gone that way; Maverick and Goose had gone, instead. Now it would be Maverick and Merlin.

"He'll fly with you. Anybody will fly with you. You're a Top Gun person now, Maverick. I'll assign him. Go get some chow and four hours' sleep, then report for preflight briefing at twenty-two-hundred hours."

"I'd . . . appreciate it if Merlin were given the choice, sir, rather than assigned."

Stinger looked at him. Maverick had had the stuffing knocked out of him, all right. He'd heard it, but he hadn't quite believed it until now. The wild one had finally been tamed. It was about time.

"All right, Maverick. I'll invite him to join you. And if he declines the invitation, we'll send somebody else. This whole ship is suddenly full of Top Guns. No problem at all."

Maverick nodded and left Stinger's office. Out in the corridor, he remembered the night Cougar had come out of this office, leaving his wings behind him on the desk. He couldn't help wondering if he'd end up going that way, too—quitting because it was the best thing for everyone else. He shuddered and put his hand up to his eyes, suddenly very tired. He turned in at the officers' mess and ate heartily, then slept a restless, troubled sleep.

Merlin showed up at the briefing, excited and gratified to be going along. He gave Maverick the thumbs-up sign as he walked into the room.

Stinger was brief and to the point: "One of our ships, a Navy oceanographic ship in international waters, was fired upon by unknown forces earlier today. The unknown forces were flying in Migs. It's our ship, and our orders are to escort it out of the area."

Stinger hit the wall map with his stick, tapping a circle around a small area. Each pilot had a copy of the same map, and sixteen pens drew the same circle with headings and vectors penciled in.

"This is bulls-eye," Stinger went on. "A rescue operation is to begin within the hour. Your mission is to give air support to that rescue. There *are* Migs in the area, and tensions are high. If you witness a hostile act, you will return fire. We will be covering three hundred sixty degrees of the compass by section. Be ready for anything."

The sixteen pairs of pilots and RIOs sat quietly, in full flight suits, listening attentively.

"Iceman and Hollywood, Sector two," Stinger called out. The two stood up, ready to go. "Maverick and Merlin, you'll back them up on Ready five."

The disappointment stung badly, but Maverick hoped it didn't have time to be seen fleeting across his face. "Yes, sir." He glanced at Iceman, the rock. The four men moved out of the ready room and up in the elevator to the flight deck. Maverick caught Iceman looking at him; it was a look of no confidence.

It was a look to bring a dead fighting spirit back to life. Maverick felt a stirring deep down in his bones. But personal feelings would have to wait; there was a job to be done and that came before anything and everything else. They stepped off the elevator onto the flight deck, where the F-14s were already rolled out and being hooked to the catapults, wheels chocked and engines ready to rev.

On the walk-around, they checked the load: two A1 M-54 A long-range Phoenix air-to-air missiles, three A1 M-7E medium-range Sparrow AAMs, two A1 M-9G H short-range Sidewinders, one M-61 A1 20-millimeter gun with 675 rounds (for *very* close-range engagement)—the maximum external load, 14,500 pounds. Launch rails and pallets in place, missile pylon cranked and ready. They climbed aboard and strapped in with practiced efficiency, not a move or gesture wasted. There was a cloud cover at about 6,000 feet, white and deceptively benign, breaking to reveal a sunny infinity of clear blue sky.

Within minutes, Iceman and Slider were catapulted off and airborne, with Hollywood and Wolfman right behind them. Maverick watched them shoot away and streak up into the clouds. As the crew maneuvered Merlin and him into takeoff position, he swore it again to himself: no feelings, nothing but the job to do, now. It was okay, he didn't think he felt much of anything. Just do the job, that was all there was. No feelings at all. Poised on the carrier deck, hooked up to Number One Catapult, blast deflector up, wings and flaps in position, he waited and listened.

Iceman: "Mustang, this is Voodoo One. We are on station."

Overhead, the two jets streaked past at 10,000 feet. They were making a circle, encompassing the wounded ship and the *Kitty Hawk*. Maverick could see them all clearly in his mind's eye—Ice and Hollywood flying together, their eyes searching the horizon, while Slider and Wolfman in the rear cockpits kept close tab on the instruments. Maverick looked back at his RIO. Merlin was concentrating deeply—on a hand-held computer game called Jet Attack. He was maneuvering the tiny buttons with his huge gloved fingers as if his life depended on the outcome.

Damn it, he missed Goose . . . but not now. No personal stuff, not now, not anything except the action. He watched his radar blips and listened to the constant radio babble: vectors and altitudes and speeds and—

"Contact. Two bogeys, twenty right. At twelve miles. Closing," Hollywood announced.

Even as he spoke, the blips appeared on the screen. "Talley-ho," Iceman confirmed. "Two Migs at two o'clock low."

Down they came, flying low to the deck, swooping over and suddenly pulling full vertical, straight up.

"What are your intentions, boys?" Hollywood asked facetiously.

Iceman made his decision. "They're just hassling," he cut in. "Let's work them out of the area."

Waiting here below was the hardest thing Maverick had ever done. He couldn't stand it. He scanned the sky and listened helplessly to the action over his head. Was it going to be as straightforward as it seemed? What were those Migs doing, anyway? Why were they hanging around? Was it to draw them in—was that why they had attacked the unarmed research ship—just to get a line on what the newest Top Guns could do? If that was the case, there had to be some surprises up there, waiting . . .

"I've got two more bogeys coming in at four o'clock high," Wolfman called out.

"Got 'em," Hollywood confirmed.

The four Migs joined together in a box formation and began to circle the area, a wider circumference that included the two ships and the two F-14s. The sounds of the jet minuet overhead grew louder and faster as the planes streaked by the carrier and disappeared once more in the distance.

"Two more—two more contacts," Hollywood reported. "Two-seven-zero at ten miles. We need some help here, Mustang."

Iceman's cold, steady voice confirmed. "Mustang, we have four Migs in the area of bulls-eye. Request you launch the Alert Five for support."

Switch on. Revving. Within seconds, Maverick got the launch order. He turned to the catapult officer, who saluted. Maverick returned the salute: all was ready. The cat officer dropped to his belly on the deck, and Maverick and Merlin felt the slam backward as they were fired off the deck to rocket into the sky.

"Roger, Voodoo." The CCA's voice came filtering through the mike.

Racing to meet them, Maverick kept his eye on the readouts projected on his windshield and listened more intently than ever to the radio talk. Something big was going on there, and finally he was to be part of it.

Two of the Migs cut scissors-fashion across the path that Iceman and Hollywood were cutting in the sky. Provoking them. Looking for trouble. Then they joined up again and flew level at ten thousand feet, within view of the Tomcats, doing tricks. One of them suddenly flopped a canopy roll.

"Very fancy!" Hollywood jeered. But then there was an ear-breaking explosion and a flash, and suddenly, out of nowhere, Hollywood was hit. *Wham!* Just that fast, he was hit and going down. His F-14 disappeared into the clouds.

Maverick couldn't believe it. He heard the explosion, he saw the plane disappear from his scanner. "Merlin, what happened?" he asked.

"Hollywood got hit," Merlin answered, sounding as stunned and bewildered as he felt.

"Wood! Wood! Acknowledge!" Iceman was repeating, over and over. And then: "I'm coming for you, Hollywood. Acknowledge, acknowledge."

Iceman put his nose down and shot through the cloud cover, reporting back to the carrier as he went: "Voodoo One, Mustang. Voodoo Three is hit. Going down. Will attempt SAR."

But when he broke through the cover at 15,000 feet, there was nothing for him to see but water. "Slider, do you have them? Did they get out or not?" Iceman asked his RIO.

"No contact. I don't know. It happened too fast," Slider answered, confused.

"Goddamn it!" That was the most emotion anyone had ever heard from Iceman. He was human, after all.

"Voodoo, Ghost Rider One. I'm on the way. Wait for me," Maverick called.

Iceman's response was bitter, cold, and sarcastic. His voice was hardly human. "Right! Watch him close, Slider."

"Roger," Slider acknowledged.

"Ghost Rider, Voodoo Three is gone," Iceman told him.

"Copy Voodoo One," Maverick acknowledged.

"Mustang. Ghost Rider. Request permission to fire." The words were icicles, honed and sharp and cold as death. They all waited, without breathing, to hear Strike's answer.

It took a moment, but then it came across. "Voodoo, Ghost Rider: this is Mustang. Cleared to fire. Cleared to fire."

And, for the first time ever, there was a hint of emotion in Iceman's voice. Low, steady, but vibrating like taut, hot wires, his words came over the mike: "Roger. Engaging. I have the lead."

Chapter 20

THE AWG-9 PHOENIX Missile System is the most effective air-to-air missile yet devised. The secret is the AWG-9 radar, which allows the F-14's radar intercept officer to track twenty-four targets simultaneously and to fire at six of them at the same time. Carrying the cannon and the Sparrow and Sidewinder missiles as well as the phenomenal Phoenix, the F-14 has the advantage over anything in the air. Once fired, the Phoenix missile is on its own, carrying its own radar guidance system, capable of penetrating the most sophisticated, known ECM jamming screens. Experts everywhere still talk about one of its earliest tests, when a QF-86 drone pulled six Gs in attempting to break lock and elude the missile—the Phoenix pulled sixteen Gs and scored.

The unique F-14 two-man fighting jet has the edge over anything in the air, but not unless the pilot gets it where the action is.

* * *

"Let's go!" Merlin whooped at Iceman's command. "Let's cream those bastards!"

Maverick had his hand on the stick. He watched Iceman swoop down, heading straight for the hornet's nest of Migs. His hand didn't move, couldn't move, for an instant. The vertical display indicator and the horizontal D.I. just below it were going crazy with blips and arrows, data skidding around like wasps on a daisy. The stick felt strange in his hand. He didn't know what to do with it.

"Come on, man! Engage! Get your nose in there!" Merlin yelped.

Again, Maverick hesitated. Cougar had quit, and didn't that make him the only sane one of them all? There was death down there, screaming and attacking and soaring in every direction, whining like a banshee and trying to pin it on him. Goose was dead, and now Hollywood and Wolfman were gone, and the whole thing was a bloody trap. Merlin might die, and how could anyone go on living if that life was on his conscience with all the others—

Merlin's voice cut into his thoughts. Dropping the excited, frantic go-get-'em enthusiasm, Merlin sounded as if he was giving an order. Quiet, deliberate, forceful, taking no crap. "Bandit at seven o'clock low—solo. Take him, Maverick."

Maverick did not respond. He couldn't engage. But he nosed the F-14 forward. Both men in the plane could see Iceman's jet surrounded by five Migs. Maverick inched a little closer, but he leveled off the plane.

"I've got radar lock!" Merlin shouted. "You are clear to fire. I repeat, clear to fire."

But Maverick just hovered there, his hand on the stick. He still couldn't engage.

Merlin twisted in his seat, frantically looking around for enemy planes on their tail. He stared at Maverick with dawning panic. "I've got radar lock! You are clear to fire."

Maverick's face was frozen under the helmet, drops of sweat forming under the foam-rubber protector. He still kept the F-14 in a hover.

Merlin was growing more and more agitated. "Repeat, Maverick. I'm locked! Shoot, shoot!"

They had come up on the tail of a Mig. Merlin could see it, set perfectly in the center of his target. But Maverick didn't shoot; he was concentrating on a speck in the distance and thinking of Goose. He couldn't shoot.

Merlin was going crazy now. "Maverick! Shoot it! I'm locked!"

The Mig ahead of them dropped slightly. Iceman's plane was now plainly visible. Maverick nudged the stick and broke the engagement. He didn't move after the enemy Mig.

Slowly and deliberately he spoke to Merlin. "I can't tell who you are locked on. Bogey and Ice are both in my gunsight."

Maverick streaked the F-14 through the field. He was taking them away from the action. Merlin froze and saw Iceman through his window. Iceman was desperately trying to escape a Mig on his six.

Slider, his eyes never leaving the radar, clenched his fists. "God damn it! Maverick is disengaging!" Slider's lips narrowed into a thin slit.

Iceman croaked back to Slider, "It figures." He was almost hissing. "Shit!"

Maverick, high in the air above Iceman, was holding something in his left hand. Merlin, straining toward his pilot, couldn't see what it was. But Maverick couldn't take his eyes off the thing he clenched and unclenched in his palm. Goose's dogtags. His gaze was frozen on them. And so was his mind. He was consumed by them, and, as long as he was, he couldn't fight. He couldn't make himself engage. Maverick thought about all that Goose had gone through with him, and how it just didn't *feel* the same without his RIO behind him. Then, all of a sudden, he realized Merlin was behind him, nervous as hell. And if it were Goose, he'd be in the thick of things now, helping Iceman out. Maverick realized he had to fly, he had to keep on fighting. Goose would've expected it of him. Dogtags still in his hand, Maverick wiped the sweat from his forehead. His right hand fingered the stick and pushed it up and forward.

Maverick's plane streaked straight up and peeled the egg. He headed down in a looping slice. They could see the Migs still tight on Iceman's plane.

Iceman screamed, "MAVERICK! How about some help here? ENGAGE, GOD DAMN IT!"

Maverick's right hand pulled the stick over sharply; the F-14 rolled in hard and fast toward the battle that was raging below them. Suddenly, the cluster of stinging wasps broke apart—now they were Migs, bogeys, enemy planes that Maverick knew what to do with. They were pulling together again, but Maverick blasted right into the middle of their formation and they scattered like roaches when the light goes on. Only for a minute though; they came back fast and mad.

A third Mig appeared through the clouds, roaring past Maverick and then banking sharply around, while another came rolling in and circled them. Before they could get out of his way, the attacking Mig had a lock on them.

Migs came from every direction, outnumbering the Tomcats and keeping them busy dodging. Suddenly gunfire erupted from one of the Migs—a new dimension to the sounds of jet engines and afterburners and radio voices. The sky glittered with the rapid-fire explosions.

Maverick acted on instinct, pure and hard. "Maverick's engaged," he reported. "Hard left, Ice. Block the eastern section."

The F-14s executed a left oblique turn in perfect unison. They came down in a section attack, cannons blazing. They were outnumbered, four Migs to two Tomcats.

From Maverick's cockpit, everything looked choppy, hard to follow, even with the heads-up display and the two screens below it showing the angles and vectors of the planes. Migs were sliding past at incredible speed, guns were blasting now from every source, and shrieking jets jockeyed for position.

Maverick and Iceman had to fight defensively; there was no other option with those odds. Maverick got the angle on a Mig and was closing in on him when Merlin spotted a missile launch. "Break left! Break left!" he shouted. "Chaft! Flares!"

"Breaking left!" Maverick responded instantly. He released a flare as he took the F-14 into a hard left turn. The deadly missile that was speeding straight at them tracked the heat of the flare instead, sailing on out of their range to the great beyond.

No time to breathe. "Two Migs on my tail, Maverick. I'm defensive," Iceman reported.

Maverick jerked the stick to the right, heading back into the fight. One of the Migs was in his sights; he cut it off with cannon fire, forcing it to evade in a downward roll. That gave Ice the room to go into vertical and come around for an angle on the second Mig that had been holding him in its grip.

"Maverick!" Slider called out from the rear cockpit of the Iceman's plane, "Six o'clock!"

As he turned to look behind him, Maverick jerked hard left. The Mig was on him, close and ugly, coughing fire from the cannon. There was no place to go, no time to do it. His front was blocked and the fire was on his six.

Iceman yo-yoed inside to cut the Mig off. Coolly and decisively, he got the pursuer in his sights and went in for the kill. "Fox one," he announced, as he let off a Sidewinder. With an abrupt, hard turn, the Mig managed to get under it, and the missile sailed on by.

"Bandit, three o'clock high!" Slider reported. Even as his words rang out, Iceman's plane was caught in a hail of cannon fire. The Mig swept down on him. Ice dived. The Mig stayed on him. They streaked across the sky, low, skimming the surface of the blue Pacific.

"Ice is defensive," Merlin said. "We gotta help him out."

Maverick nodded and nosed down to get a sighting on the two planes chasing across the horizon. He caught up with them and intercepted, forcing the bogey to look away from Iceman and pay attention to him, instead.

"Reverse right," Maverick told Iceman. Ice turned right, the Mig opted out, and jerked into vertical. Up and away—with Maverick close behind.

"Stay with him," Merlin reported. "Your six is clear."

Maverick closed on the Mig, jerking left, right, twisting and turning, staying on his tail no matter how the bogey tried to evade and break away.

"One on our six! Bug out! Bug out!"

Bullets flew past them from the Mig that had suddenly appeared on their tail. Maverick pulled a hard left, then a vertical, straight up. With Merlin shouting instructions from his readouts, the battle closed in again and all six planes were hard at it, circling and dodging and spitting death at each other.

Maverick broke free at one moment and soared vertical again, gaining a vantage point from which he could peel over the top and come down on the Migs like a jungle cat. With the advantage he gained by the surprise tactic, he made a series of passes at the Migs. It seemed to confuse them; he thought he had them on the run.

"Okay, going up," he announced. "Ice, go high."

"Look out!" Iceman shouted.

A Mig was coming down on them from above, its belly obscenely visible, too close, too close . . . collision course!

"Jesus . . ." Maverick swore—or prayed.

He pushed down, and the Mig roared by, missing them by a mere four or five feet. The F-14 shook from nose to tails—it was that close. The air-pressure shock wave slammed them as it went by. "Ohhhh shit!" Merlin groaned.

It hurt, all through flesh and bones and tissue and nerves. It ached and pinched and contracted the organs in a hell of a cramp. But there was no time to worry about it. Down below, a Mig was trying to bug out and go home; Iceman was on his six. The Mig maneuvered, jerking hard left, then hard right, twisting up and then down. But Ice stayed right in his shadow. They came in fast and low over the water.

He had the Mig in the diamond. From above, riding cover, Maverick and Merlin held their breath, knowing what the Iceman was going to do.

"Good tone. Fox two," he reported. No emotion. The Sidewinder shot forward from his pylon.

The Mig executed a fast turn. The missile went by his tail. "Son of a bitch!" Iceman shouted, but the rarified sound of his fury was cut off sharply by the ear-twisting sound of metal crunching. The Mig started to break up before their eyes, almost in slow motion for the first minute or two. The tail came off, and the plane rolled over. Starting to fall rapidly, the fuselage erupted suddenly, spinning away the canopy like a Frisbee gone berserk. The pilot ejected. He cleared the falling, spinning plane and his chute opened, just as the Mig exploded into thousands of small pieces. The pilot hung in his straps, drifting down toward the debris that had been his plane.

Iceman flew by him. "Jesus! Splash one, splash one bandit!" Slider shouted excitedly. "Splash that sucker! We did it, Ice—"

"I've got one here. On the nose," Maverick cut in. "Coming down."

His Sidewinder was sounding a perfect tone; the bogey was his. The Migs sensed him, and they broke, with one swooping down low to meet him.

"On the nose?" Iceman repeated, as if he didn't believe it.

"Got 'em," Maverick confirmed. "Got good tone." He squeezed the trigger.

The missile fired, the vapor trail coming off. The Mig turned as though he'd been bounced off a rubber wall, came around on the missile, and, incredibly, beat it. The missile flew by him.

"Ah, shit, shit, shit!" Maverick groaned. "Goddamn it!"

The Mig came back, turning toward him, mad. Maverick was poised to try again, with an eye on the left side console and its target-designate switches. The radar tone would tell him when. And there it was . . . almost in the diamond.

"There's another one up there . . ." Merlin reported.

"I got one coming up!" Maverick protested.

". . . and he's gunning," Merlin added urgently.

Maverick looked back. Thirty-millimeter tracers were whipping by, but at the speed the F-14 was traveling, the bullets seemed to be almost lazily floating past. He broke and dived, hit the airbrakes, and got out of the way. The trailing Mig kept going.

No time to go on the offensive again; there was another bogey coming straight for him. They closed at 900 knots—*vaboom!!!!*—passing nose-to-nose, canopy-to-canopy. Both planes pitched straight up, trying for the altitude advantage.

"Zone five burners," Maverick called out.

He hit the afterburners and the F-14 outclimbed the Mig easily. Rearing back on its tails, full-thruster, it rocketed straight up, away from the planet. Maverick had the advantage. He felt like himself again, faster and higher and on top of it all . . . and then it all collapsed. Merlin was the first to call it.

"We're ballistic! Ohhhhhh, shit . . ."

The plane backed down on itself, into its own smoke, as it flipped over and fell away. Maverick grabbed the stick, reached firmly for the controls on the left side instrument console—throttle quadrant, G-valve push button, servopneumatic altimeter, vertical velocity indicator. Slowly, the plane began to respond. Maverick had it under control, straightening out, starting to behave, when a roar from above hooked his attention. The Mig was right on him, filling the canopy, darkening the sky.

Chapter 21

MERLIN SWIVELED AND saw the Mig bearing down on them. It was a terrifying sight, that speeding jet, coming right toward them.

Pushing to miss the bogey's attack, Maverick broke fast, downward. And, in a precisely choreographed maneuver, Maverick swung out and back up, swiftly, pinning Merlin to his seat. Merlin felt like his spine would crack in two. But Maverick, if insane, was back in control. His face was plastered with a huge grin.

In a few minutes, they were flying alongside the Iceman again.

Ice was trying to shake a Mig that was flicking around him like a gnat in July, teasing, dancing, at 300 knots. Maverick rolled in on them. The Mig hadn't been expecting to see him again—for an instant he presented a perfect target, but he ducked around to keep Iceman between them.

"Did you plan this whole thing for a surprise?" Merlin asked in awe. "Was that whole fucking maneuver something you fucking *planned?*"

181

Maverick was all business. "All right, Ice," he radioed. "Come hard starboard, then extend same direction."

It was taking Merlin awhile to recover. "Because, if that was . . . next time you *tell* me first. Okay?"

"Roger." Maverick fell back while Ice tried to get starboard of the Mig. He zoomed out fast, taking the Mig the other way. Maverick yo-yoed in, coming right up behind the Mig, which started acceleration. "I've got a winder left," Maverick reported, "but no good tone on it."

"I can't lose him. Can you get off a shot?" Iceman asked.

"I got no tone. It might get you."

"Go for it," Iceman told him. "Shoot it!"

"When I shoot, you break left," Maverick said. "Three . . . two . . ." The Mig cannon started to spit at him before he had a chance to push the button. "He fired!" Maverick shouted. "Break now!"

Ice broke left and dropped flares. The Mig's missile followed the flares. Maverick fired the Sidewinder.

The missile didn't twitch. It flew right up the tailpipe of the Mig. The canopy flew off, the pilot shot out of it, and then the Mig exploded into a mammoth fireball, making noises like the lower rungs of Hell.

"He's out! We got him!" Maverick yelled.

The blazing Mig rolled down and down, straight into the sea, sending up a skewer of steam and vapor and then nothing, until debris started to float up. The two F-14s swooped down to go by the pilot, hanging in his straps. Merlin waved at him. "Happy landing!" he called out. "Get another plane, we'll be happy to shoot you down again. That's what we're here for!"

In perfect formation, Maverick and Iceman joined up, lit the fire, and stood on their burners, blasting straight for the sun. Then, without warning, Maverick fell away, rolling over—and over—and over.

"Oh, my God, what is it? What's wrong?" Merlin cried out. He started checking his circuit breakers, all instruments, all indicators, readouts, scanners. But now they were straight again, rejoining Iceman, smooth. "Is there something I should know?" he asked tentatively.

"Just relax," Maverick told him.

"Is it the plane?"

"The plane is fine."

"Is it you?"

"No." Maverick chuckled. To the RIO's great relief, they leveled and started to climb again. "Hey, Merlin, I want you to do me a little favor."

"Sure," Merlin answered, resigned to flying with a crazy man.

Maverick got on the UHF. "Hello, Mustang, this is Maverick. I've got a message for Stinger."

"Roger, Maverick. Go ahead," Strike answered.

"Tell Stinger that Maverick has good news and bad news. The good news is that Iceman got a Mig. The bad news is that Maverick got two!" He couldn't help grinning as he looked over at Iceman.

Iceman nodded. "Music to my ears, Maverick. Nice flying," he said.

Maverick threw back his head in relief and a kind of thank-you gesture. "We gotta have one," he said.

Iceman only took a second to figure out what he meant, then he nodded and Maverick was almost positive he was smiling under his mask. But Slider cut in with practical considerations. "I don't know, Ice," his RIO said, "we've really been burning up the fuel."

Ice considered this for a moment. "I know," he acknowledged coolly. "I know."

"You're not supposed to," Merlin warned.

"But I have to! I got a reputation to uphold," Maverick pointed out.

"Well . . . since you put it that way." Merlin was acknowledging a whole lot of things in that acquiescence—forgiving Maverick all, and they both knew it.

"Mustang, this is Maverick. Request a flyby."

The reaction in the primary flight control room back on the USS *Kitty Hawk* could only be imagined. After a moment or two in which all kinds of interesting hell must have broken loose, the air boss got on the mike. "Ghost Rider, the pattern's full."

Another moment passed. Then Iceman called in. "Mustang, this is Voodoo One. Request a flyby for two."

The mike was open and they heard someone say, "Who is that guy?"

There was no mistaking the admiral's deep, commanding basso as he replied, "That's the Top Gun."

"Both of them," came Stinger's proud claim, loud and clear. He must have left the mike open deliberately; Stinger didn't make mistakes. And he must have known how it would come out. Maverick looked over at Ice, who signaled "thumbs-up."

"Boss, you better clear it out. We're five minutes out and we're doing it!" Maverick crowed. He pictured them all—admiral, air boss, Stinger, all the officers and crew looking for cover on the flight deck so as not to miss it—and not to get hit with it. Maverick laughed to himself. Life was wonderful. At any rate, it had its moments.

"Ten miles astern, boss," he reported.

"Mustang to Ghost Rider!" His voice was tight.

But something happened back on the pri-fly bridge, and Maverick was willing to bet it was the admiral giving them the nod. Because a truly pissed-off air boss was saying, "Roger, Ghost Rider, you're clear."

Sailors lined the deck, searching the sky. They craned their necks from their battle stations, sweating in the sun, watching for the double approach. Someone spotted them and gave a shout, heads turned and every eye strained to catch the sight. Then they appeared— two F-14s in tandem, perfect unison flying, coming down like pinpoints out of the blue.

"Now?" Merlin asked.

"Now!" Maverick agreed.

"Great balls of fire!" Merlin shouted.

They came screaming in, five feet over the water, throwing up rooster tails behind, heading straight for the *Kitty Hawk* at 500 knots. At the last millisecond, they split off, zooming along either side of the carrier at an altitude of one hundred feet. That brought Maverick close enough to the pri-fly bridge to see the whites of the AB's eyes—he could only imagine the joy within. The walls must have warped from the noise, dust sifting from the overhead . . . maybe he actually knocked the air boss off his big duck feet.

Laughing, Maverick turned and watched Iceman take his flyby. This time he saw the tower shake, for sure. It was delicious. He saw the sailors and crews running out now, and they were cheering and waving as they set about getting the hooks ready for them. The two planes joined up and rolled back for the landing, braking down to 128 knots.

Iceman took the first shot at the ramp and was waved in. He came in a little rockily, bouncing hard but grabbing the first wire, jerking to a sudden stop. The sailors were cheering, all right, and throwing victory fists up in the air as they strained to get a look at Iceman, while his crew directed his plane off to the side. Opening the canopy, Ice and Slider unstrapped. Stinger and the other officers were there, and guys were climbing all over the airplane. They started painting a Mig on the side, not even waiting for it to cool down.

Maverick came in and heard the same roar of applause and cheers—music. Pilots in flight suits poured from the deck hatch, the ground crew swarmed all over them, sailors shouted, and the paint crew couldn't wait to start the illustrations. Climbing down, Maverick couldn't believe his eyes—amid the swarms of guys, two faces he never thought he'd see again: Hollywood and Wolfman . . .

They were walking off the forward elevator. Maverick caught a glimpse of smoke-stained canopy and oil-smeared wingtip as the elevator began its descent to the hangar deck with their battle-damaged plane aboard. He worked his way through the congratulatory crowd and caught up with them.

"What happened to you?" he asked, pounding them on the shoulders. They were really there, alive and kicking! Hollywood had his hair mussed and a streak of dirt was on his pretty face. Wolfman looked like a stuffed toy that had gotten tossed in the washing machine by mistake. Nobody had ever looked so good to Maverick.

"Oh, we just hit a curb, parking, that's all," Wolfman told him.

"You are two lucky guys," Maverick said.

"Not luck," Hollywood said, shaking his head. *"Skill."*

The commotion on deck tempered as the crews got busy securing the planes and taking them downstairs for the deep inspections and maintenance. The fliers started going below to the ready room, to change out of their flight suits and head for debriefing. When Maverick walked into the ready room, Iceman eyed him for a long minute with the same old cold-fish stare. Then he surprised everyone by flashing a smile that seemed actually friendly.

"I guess I owe you one," he said loudly enough for everyone to hear.

"You don't owe me anything," Maverick told him. He went over to his old locker, with his name still on it. He started getting out of the harness.

Iceman persisted. "You saved our lives. You did it."

Maverick smiled. He actually liked the guy, all of a sudden. *"We* did it," he said. "We're on the same team."

Iceman spread his arms wide and first thing he knew, Maverick was being hugged by the guy. "You can be my wingman any time," Iceman told him.

Maverick laughed and pulled back. "Bullshit!" he hollered. "You can be *mine!"*

Everybody laughed, including the Iceman. Nobody was ever going to win this one. It would stay a running joke between them. The two Top Guns.

"Whatever you say, Commander," Ice sang out. He snapped to in a proud salute, which Slider instantly copied, standing at attention with his pants down around his ankles. Maverick, grinning, quickly returned the salute. He was really proud, until Ice and Slider snapped it off, turning the tribute into the "pilot's salute," and giving him the bird. That felt better, more normal. Laughing, Maverick and Merlin returned the compliment.

Maverick was the last one out of the ready room, deliberately. After all the hoopla and the pride, the jokes and kidding around, he wanted time out. He sat down on the bench and looked up at the door of the locker next to his. Nobody had removed the adhesive tape with the name written on it: *Lt. Nick Bradshaw "GOOSE."*

He stared at it for a long time, thinking, remembering. What he remembered were good times, happy and foolish moments, a friend. He swung the locker open—they had emptied it out but had forgotten to take off the name. Slowly, he reached up and pulled off the tape.

Stinger found him there. "Hey, Mig killer! I've been looking for you. I've got news that's going to make you very happy. You've got the big duty option, Maverick. You pulled it off—the sky's the limit! Anything, anyplace. What do you think you'll go for, son?"

Maverick rolled the adhesive into a tight wad in his fist. He grinned back at Stinger. "Mig killer. What else is there?"

Later, alone again, he went up to the flight deck, to the railing at the bow of the ship. He looked down at the sharp point plowing through the deepening blue water, churning up foam and fury below. He opened his hand, unknotted the adhesive tape, and carefully stretched it out on the ship's rail. *Lt. Nick Bradshaw*

"GOOSE." He laid it straight and then, starting at one end, he rolled it up neatly, carefully, with reverence. Then, taking Goose's dogtags out of his pocket and looking at them one last time, he threw both into the sea.

Chapter 22

"You're here because you are the top one percent of all Navy aviators. You're the elite, the best of the best. We're going to make you better, because your job is damned important."

Viper's words were familiar, but the faces lined up in rapt attention before him were new—the best and the brightest, fresh young hotshots ready to die for a chance to prove how good they were.

Viper's powerful voice rang out over the room. "In the back of this room stands your enemy—your instructors." When the heads turned to scan the line behind them, they saw those who taught the best of the best. Relaxed, poised, and mean, they stood in a line along the back wall of the room. Maverick was among them, unsmiling as he looked over the class, picking out which were the hotshots, the troublemakers, the potentially greats. Takes one to know one, he thought to himself.

"Photographs of all of them are stored in the war room of the Kremlin," Viper barked. "Some of them are Mig killers. Let me assure you, they fly dirty."

Maverick spotted him—the one like himself. Checking out the competition. Briefly, the flier made eye contact with Maverick. Maybe he recognized the same thing. He looked away and Maverick's lip skewed into a crooked little half-smile. He was going to love this.

"You will be trained and evaluated by a few civilian specialists as well," Viper told the new class. It struck a harmonic chord somewhere in Maverick's gut, but he wasn't one to dwell on the past. "These civilians are here because they are the very best sources on enemy aircraft as well as current battle air warfare techniques. I'd like to introduce our TAGREP . . ." Maverick's breathing quickened. He looked up. Viper was pointing to a Harvard type in jeans and sport jacket. "Jim Keeton," Viper announced.

The force of the disappointment surprised him. He certainly had not expected *her,* but just for that minute . . . with Viper's speech being the same, it seemed to him maybe other things could be the same, too . . . but forget it. Okay, it was forgotten.

"Gentlemen, this school is about combat. Remember," Viper concluded, "there are no points for second place."

Later that day, Maverick, alone again, found himself at a bar, having a beer. It was the same bar he'd gone to with Goose that first night on the town. The same bar where he'd met Charlie. The bar was deserted, but suddenly the jukebox came on, softly. It was a Righteous Brothers song. Maverick looked into his beer and thought how ironic it was. It was the same song he and Goose had sung in front of Charlie that night. He mouthed the words now, silently. Then he looked over at the jukebox. No one was there—but if no one was there, who had . . . Maverick smiled, got up from his barstool and walked toward the machine. He leaned against it, his hands in his pockets.

Suddenly, there was a voice behind him, a familiar voice. He turned around. And there she was, Charlie, leaning in the doorjamb, beautiful as ever.

"Hi, Pete Mitchell," she said, her eyes smiling at him.

"You back here for a while?" he asked as casually as he could manage.

Charlie nodded. "Yep. They gave me the Big Option. Anywhere. I took Perry's job."

Maverick was going to move closer. "This could be complicated," Maverick said with a sigh.

"Yep."

"The first time I crashed and burned."

"And the second?" beautiful Charlie said, unwinding his heart completely.

"I'll tell you tomorrow, but it's looking good so far." His arms opened for her, and yes, the kiss was as wonderful as he remembered, and all the rest of their lives was a real possibility, now.